BLOOD
RUNNER

For Helen

Text copyright © James Riordan 2011
The right of James Riordan to be identified as the author
of this work has been asserted by him in accordance with the
Copyright, Designs and Patents Act, 1988 (United Kingdom).

First published in Great Britain in 2011 and in the USA in 2012 by
Frances Lincoln Children's Books, 4 Torriano Mews,
Torriano Avenue, London NW5 2RZ
www.franceslincoln.com

A catalogue record for this book is available from
the British Library.

ISBN: 978-1-84507-934-5

Set in PalatinoTT

Printed and bound by CPI Group (UK) Ltd, Croydon, CR0 4YY
in August 2011

9 8 7 6 5 4 3 2 1

James
Riordan

BLOOD
RUNNER

The long race
to freedom

F

FRANCES LINCOLN
CHILDREN'S BOOKS

This is a fictional story, not a biography. It follows one man's struggle for freedom in Apartheid South Africa during the years before Nelson Mandela's release from prison. Many of the events portrayed actually happened. The characters, however, are entirely fictional.

The book is inspired in part by Josiah Thugwane, the first black South African to win an Olympic gold medal. It is dedicated to all South Africans, black and white, who fought to bring justice and freedom to their country.

What does one do and
where does one go
when one feels the rough,
the excesses of racism?

Where does one find love
in a comfortless world,
intoxicated with
hatred and racial intolerance?

Where human progress is
suppressed
by denial and ignorance?

Monde Tinzi, aged 16
Oscar Mpetha High School, Nyanga,
Western Cape

Prologue

It's a misty, steamy morning as over a hundred runners jostle their way into the empty stadium. Hoarse voices and shuffling feet echo round the concrete bowl and up the rows of seats, to fade like smoke in the early dawn. Back down from the great oval of sky comes the cawing of crows, unnaturally harsh: *Ker-raw-w-wak! Ker-raw-w-wak!*

On the red-brick track, spindly legs twitch nervously. Edgy fingers hover over stopwatch buttons. Anxious eyes fix the time: 6.57. A few minutes to go. One hundred and twenty-three men prepare to run 26 miles 385 yards.

Among the runners is a small, slight, black man. The new rainbow nation of South Africa has sent two experienced white runners and an untried black man to the Olympic Games. Since he ranks a lowly 41st in the marathon world, everyone agrees that he is just there as a token black runner. Mark his card an odds-on DNF (Did Not Finish).

The young black runner's nerves jingle-jangle like

cracked church bells as he waits for the starter's gun. Ahead lie miles and miles, and more miles. He'll do his best, but in his heart of hearts he knows he has little chance of a medal.

If only his knees would stop knocking and his hands trembling! *Settle down, boy.* Trying to calm himself, he lets his thoughts drift far away. To his childhood. To his family. Back to that fateful day. . .

CHAPTER ONE

It seems so long ago now. Yet it is fresh in his mind, part of his whole being. He can see and hear it still, smell and touch it. It is as real, as bitter-sweet as running.

For Samuel, running always rakes over the dust of the past, exposing the pain and joy of what lies beneath his feet.

First the joy. The joy of small, bare feet with leathery soles pitter-pattering on the dusty township road, chasing strutting pigeons until they flap away, flopping down several hops behind him, racing helter-skelter at the head of a bunch of shrieking kids.

'Faster, faster! Catch me if you can!' he'd yell as he burst ahead, teasing them by slowing down, pretending to be out of wind. When they'd almost caught him, he would twist and turn away from them again with a laugh.

No matter how they tried, they couldn't catch the little scamp as he led them a merry dance, along the road and out on to the baked scrubland. The young boy was the Pied Piper, dragging a straggly column behind him into the wilderness.

'Watch out for *strepies* and mambas!' he'd shout. 'Don't tread on their tails!'

That would scare the timid ones, causing them to stop and look round for striped rats and the deadly mamba. It put an extra spring in the step of the bolder among them, who tried to stick as close to the leader as they could.

Young Samuel was careful not to stray too far from the beaten track, for fear of scorpions and puff adders in the open country. He'd run in a circle, meeting the township road beside a clear, bubbling stream where the runners took a breather, cooling their hot bodies and slaking their thirst. For the moment the boy was 'King of the Road'. He might come last at hopscotch, lose all his knucklebones and marbles, be bowled out first ball against the long-drop door wicket. But when it came to running, he was a champion among the township kids.

It was the same at school. Whenever Sports Day came round, Samuel entered all the running events, even the three-legged, sack, and egg-and-spoon races. When he was on his own, no one could touch him.

So fast-footed was he, that the neighbourhood relied on him to be their alarm runner. Whenever there were rumours of a police raid, it was Samuel's job to race round and warn squatters, hooch-brewers, pass-less vagabonds and other illegals to beat it quick, before the police came knocking down doors and smashing windows. Those poor black constables could never work out who was spoiling their fun and messing up their arrest quotas. If they'd got their hands on the boy, they would have wrung his neck like a chicken. But Sam was always too fast for them.

Running was what he was good at. Not only did it give him 'street cred' among his friends, it made him happy. He loved running free across the veld, exploring different parts of the township, waving to Indian, Coloured and Black families as he passed them.

These were the images that filled his head before the start of a race. But there were other, darker images, too – images he couldn't disentangle from the brighter thoughts.

● ● ●

It was a peaceful autumn morning. The air was drowsy with jasmine and honeysuckle, the golden sun smiled down like a proud mother on her sleeping infants. Even the ever-hungry pie-dogs were dozing in the shade with half an eye on the strutting crows. Whenever a bird stepped too close, a low, sleepy growl sent it scuttling off.

It was holiday time. School was closed and men had a day off from the mines. No doubt, that Monday witnessed the same scene in a thousand townships.

Yet there was something different about this Monday and this township. Something was in the air. Samuel couldn't see or hear or smell it. But he could feel it – stick out his tongue and taste the tingle, the thrill of excitement. It jiggled and tiggled all the way down to his toes.

Something was about to happen. . .

What was it? No one really knew.

You could tell by the knowing looks – the winks and smiles – that the boy's two older brothers, Looksmart and Nicodemus, were giving each other at breakfast, that they were clearly in on the secret. Finally, their father lost patience with them.

'Come on, out with it,' he growled. 'You've been

6

walking round like hungry hyenas. I'll have no secrets in this house!'

'You won't like it, Dad,' said Looksmart, who was the oldest.

'How can I know whether I like it or not, if I don't know it?' their dad said.

Looksmart glanced from his younger brother Nicodemus to his mother, from young Samuel to little Sally. They were all sitting expectantly at the wooden table.

'Well . . . as far as I know . . . some fellows are going to the police station to protest about passes. . .'

His father snorted.

'I knew it! Hotheads looking for trouble. I don't hold with breaking the law!'

'Hold on, Dad,' said Looksmart. 'Those "hotheads", as you call them, are going peacefully to the station. They aren't going to cause any trouble. All they want to do is hand in their passbooks.'

His father snorted again, louder this time, with a 'Huh!' thrown in for good measure.

'They aren't breaking the law,' added Nicodemus. 'It's a peaceful protest, like the peace marchers in England. Surely someone has to do something about the unjust pass system?'

He threw in a mention of the English peace marchers for his father's benefit, knowing how much he respected all things English. But his father only sniffed: they didn't carry passes in England, so that didn't count.

'Fat lot of good that'll do,' he grumbled. 'The police won't listen. They'll just laugh in their faces, then chuck them into gaol. Serve 'em right, if you ask me.'

'Oh, Albert, don't be such a defeatist.'

It was their mother, the rebel of the family. If she had her way, she'd brain the whole police force with her frying pan.

She went on: 'It's about time someone did something. That pass is just a badge of slavery. What should we do? Just stand there and take their insults? *"Ja, baas. Nee, baas. Dankie, baas!"* For Heaven's sake, man, where's your pride?'

Her husband shook his grizzled head.

Sam's mother had her way, as usual. So now the children could all go and watch the show. Their father was coming too, if only to make sure they didn't get up to any mischief.

'Sally, put on your blue frock. And you, Samuel, wear a clean T-shirt and your grey shorts.' This was their Sunday best – their European clothes.

Since Sally and her young brother had no shoes, they wore their tattered *takkies*.

Father wore a collar and tie under his much-darned black suit, the one he wore to church. As for Sam's mother, she disliked her husband's European tastes and refused to wear her go-to-church straw hat with its faded cherries. Instead, she swathed a headscarf round her head, tribal fashion.

The protest outside the police station was scheduled for one o'clock. So, at a quarter past twelve, the Gqibela family set off to walk to the white fort.

It was like going round the world in a single mile. You had to cross three continents of colour: Indian, Coloured and Black, each with its own district. Being 'Bantu natives', as white people called them, the blacks had the slums all to themselves. Sam's family lived in a higgledy-piggledy sprawl of dingy shacks with leaky tin roofs. The floor was bare earth covered here and there with cardboard. No running water, no gas, no electricity, no toilet – everyone used the 'long-drop' lavatory at the end of the row.

The family walked through the Indian quarter, where most people did their shopping. It was a teeming, buzzing, sweet-smelling maze of colourful emporia. Shopkeepers called out to Sam's parents, 'Come on in, Mama! Come in, sir! *Lo makulu chipile!* All very cheap!'

If you had money, you could buy anything, from a fistful of sugar cane to a goose-wing brush.

Samuel's father much preferred the respectable Coloured neighbourhood. It was clean and tidy with rows of bungalows, each with a tiny garden at front and back. No shops, no cinema bioscope, no drinking *shebeens* – just the occasional office or surgery for doctors and dentists.

As Sam's mother often said, 'We Africans are as black as ebony and as poor as church mice. If anyone else was at the bottom of a mine, they'd still be looking down on us!'

The Apartheid system was all very puzzling for a young boy. He knew that some whites worked at the police station. They were the ones who carried guns. But where did they go at night?

'Where do whites live?' Samuel asked, as they neared the station.

His father waved a hand airily towards some far-off horizon.

'But why do we live here and they live there?'

'That's how it is,' said his mother. 'Still,' she

continued with a smile, 'Old Mother Sunshine is shining today on black and white alike. And if God is up in heaven, he'll be looking down on all his children. No Apartheid there – even though those whites claim God is a white man fighting off the black devil!'

Dad was silent, but he gave his wife a look that said: *Wash your mouth out with soap and water!*

Samuel waved to his friends as they walked. It seemed that the entire township was going to watch the fun. Like many tributaries of a mighty river, families flowed into the broad stream of bodies – babbling, eddying, whirling about.

Behind the crowd ran a pack of dogs, followed by a hopping, darting congregation of shiny black crows on the look-out for scraps. They might just be in luck, for some families had brought food to have a picnic.

CHAPTER
TWO

The crowd was cracking jokes, laughing and giggling excitedly. Now and then someone shouted out a slogan – *Izwe lethu! Afrika!* 'Land to the People!' – or gave the thumbs-up freedom sign. There must have been five thousand people rolling along in the same direction.

As the Gqibela family came in sight of the police station, Mother ushered them to a sandy ridge where they could sit and look down from a safe distance. They watched a police car drive slowly past, evidently on the look-out for troublemakers. But since no one was throwing stones or clods of earth, no one was calling the police names, and no one seemed to be in charge, the police were disappointed. For all the world it resembled a church outing, especially when someone struck up a hymn and others joined in:

'Onward Christian so-ol-diers, marching as to war,
With the cross of Jee-suss going on before. . .'

The Gqibela family were sitting on the sandy hilltop enjoying their picnic. All at once, they heard the ominous crunching sound of Saracen tanks. They watched keenly as an armoured convoy headed for the police compound. Samuel laughed, and waved to the white policemen sitting on the tanks holding Sten guns and rifles.

'You'd think they were on safari, hunting bull elephants,' said his brother Nicky.

A couple of policemen waved back, grinning.

'It's fun, isn't it?' piped up Sally.

The convoy of tanks and trucks rumbled on until it reached the iron gates. There the tanks swung round to face the crowd. Some of the police began to set up heavy Browning machine guns in the station yard, while the grey lead car drove on into the inner compound.

Samuel's eyes grew wide as he took in the unfolding scene. The police were climbing inside their Saracens, battening down the hatches and peering at the crowd through slits in the armour plating. With the extra officers and guns brought in from round about, the station force had swollen to about four hundred men, armed with enough weapons to wage a war.

It was the usual bluff – a show of strength to make sure the blacks knew who was boss. Sam continued to play ball with his sister, men and women were walking arm-in-arm in and out of the crowd, people were tagging on, filled with curiosity.

Then came a drone that grew to a roar. Out of the blue sky, from over the horizon, flew a squadron of fighter planes, like a swarm of angry wasps. As they approached, they flew so low that the crowd could see the pilots inside them. Sam had never seen a fighter plane before. How kind of the Big Baas to treat them to this rip-roaring fly-past!

Despite the tanks and planes, the protesters felt they couldn't lose face by backing down now. Dead on one o'clock, the young men in T-shirts and jeans linked arms and started walking slowly towards the station. About twenty yards from the tanks, they halted and began chanting, 'No Pass! No Pass!'

Others took up the chant and added a new one – in Afrikaans, for the whites' benefit: *'Ons dak nie! Ons dak nie!* We won't move!' Quietly, nervously at first. Then louder and in chorus. But it fell on deaf ears.

Nothing happened. No police emerged from the tanks or the station. Perhaps they were having a lie-in or enjoying their usual 'beer and *brai*'.

The young protesters didn't know what to do next. Sam was half hoping they'd burn their pass books or do something daredevilish so that he could cheer them on.

Then, all at once, a long line of black policemen dressed smartly in khaki shirts and shorts came filing through the iron gates. Unusually, they were carrying rifles. They were being marshalled by a white officer in a shiny peaked cap, barking, 'Left, right! Left, right! Halt!'

At his order, they lined up against the wall and gates on either side of the tanks.

'Order arms!' yelled the officer. 'Get ready to fire!'

The crowd watched, bemused, as the police pointed their rifles at the protestors.

'They're kidding, aren't they?' said Looksmart. 'They haven't even rigged up wires to a loudspeaker to give a warning, as they usually do.'

You could tell by the sweaty faces of the policemen that they were jittery. They probably saw themselves as the thin khaki line between a raging black mob and white 'civilised' society.

Samuel felt more excited than scared. He'd never seen Africans stand up to policemen before. He thought the six young men were incredibly brave. You could have cut the air with a knife. All eyes were on the young lads holding out their passes.

'Now they'll get a right ticking-off,' whispered Mother.

'Or spend a night in the cells,' hissed Father. 'That'll bring them to their senses.'

No one said a word. The sweating policemen stood like statues. The tanks, their guns trained on the crowd, were ready for action. The six protestors kept their distance, defiant and silent. One side held guns, the other passbooks.

As if in tune with the sombre mood below, dark clouds suddenly gathered overhead, spoiling what had been a crystal-clear Highveld morning. In the distance came a soft roll of thunder.

What came next was completely unexpected.

A shot rang out. Or was it a crack of thunder?

Everyone looked round. Had some rowdy in the crowd let off his pistol in the air?

The police started to panic. There were shouts of '*Daar was 'n skiet!* There was a shot!' and a hoarse command: '*Skiet!* Shoot!' – from where, no one knew.

Then all hell broke loose. The police opened fire with everything they had: pistols, rifles, Sten guns, heavy machine guns. . . There was no warning, no volley into the air. No *'Staan of ons skiet!* 'Stop, or we'll shoot!'

Toc-toc-toc-toc. Toc-toc-toc-toc. On and on and on. A hail of bullets in a thunder-burst, sharp and deep-throated, rained first into the face of the crowd, then into their backs as they turned to flee.

All in the space of a frozen minute.

At first, a few people giggled nervously, crying out *'Izwe lethu!'* They thought the police were firing blanks. The air was thick with screams and groans.

As if to dull the pain, a sudden downpour soaked police and victims alike, leaving red puddles all over the ground.

The Gqibela family watched in horror as people below them scrambled to their feet, turned round and ran for dear life. Bullets were flying everywhere. Bodies were falling. People were screaming, 'Help me!'

'Better clear up the picnic plates,' said Sam's mother urgently. It seemed an odd thing to say, in the circumstances.

People were rooted to the spot in terror. They saw

one man running towards the police, crying 'Stop! Stop! That's enough!' His shouts died in his throat as a second volley cut him down.

The bullets sprayed far and wide. One woman was hit as she drank tea in her garden; another was shot in the back hanging out the washing in her backyard hundreds of yards away. An old man had his head blown off as he cycled round the streets delivering bills. The cycle, with its headless rider, tottered on before bumping into an old lady.

Hundreds of children below Sam, hardly taller than the grass, were leaping about like rabbits. One was holding a broken black umbrella, trying to protect his head from the bullets. Some children went down and did not get up again.

'We'd better make tracks,' muttered Samuel's father, who couldn't believe what was happening. The shooting didn't seem real. Surely he thought, it was some sort of dress rehearsal for a war or gangster movie, and, unlike those who were pretending to be shot, he hadn't been let in on the act. That must be it. Why else would a white policeman on top of a Saracen be firing his Sten gun from the hip, sweeping the crowd from side to side like a Chicago gangster? Two black policemen were on the tank with him, firing pistols. *Rat-tat-tat-tat. Pop-pop-pop.*

If it was a film, most of the extras were lying on the road at the foot of the hill where Sam's family was sitting. And now the bullets were steadily climbing the hill. A man just below them fell: for a moment he lay dazed, stood up, walked a few paces towards them, his hands held out. Then he fell flat on his face.

The guns found their range. Mother was the first to fall. Then Sally. As Father stooped to help them, he shooed the other children on: 'Run, children. Run for your lives! For Christ's sake!'

Those were his last words. For this was no movie. This was real. Dead real. Mother, Sally – and now Father. Like the others, he'd been shot in the back. For a moment Samuel stared at his body as it jerked and squirmed in the dust; it slowly grew still, the arms reaching out for his wife and daughter. A dark red stain quickly spread over the jacket of his best suit.

Samuel never forgot the look on his father's face. It was as if a terrible truth had dawned on him, too late, far too late. Where was British justice now?

● ● ●

Numb with fear, Sam saw through a veil of tears a blur of jumbled colour: the orange of his mother's headscarf, the blue of Sally's dress and the black of his father's faded suit.

He looked down the hill. The police had put away their guns and were *sjambokking* anyone within reach, chasing them as they fled for shelter to a nearby church. Samuel ran as fast as his legs would carry him, outpacing his brothers and the police. He felt like a frightened hare keeping ahead of the fox, darting first one way, then the other – but always fast enough to avoid capture. He surprised himself: his speed was now saving him as never before. Down the hill, across scrubland, up the road. There was the Regina Mundi church. Almost there now. He'd be safe inside.

Words from Sunday School beat a rhythm in his head: 'Suffer the little children to come unto me.'

'I'm coming, Lord,' his brain replied.

All at once, a grim thought made him pause. Perhaps the Lord didn't have black children in mind.

CHAPTER THREE

Samuel must have passed out. For when he came to, he felt cold stone beneath him. An unfamiliar smell gave no clue to where he was. Eerie silence punctured by occasional low groans added to his confusion.

He kept his eyes screwed shut. Blindly he felt his face, head, arms, chest, legs, all the way down to his toes. No pain. No sticky fingers or thumbs.

A dazzling light pierced his eyelids and he heard a heavy door open. Through slit eyes he peered out.

He was sitting on a tiled floor. Beyond the church doors was a veritable battlefield littered with hundreds of unlaced shoes, ragged trousers, hats, mangled bicycles, walking sticks and a few umbrellas. Scores of twisted bodies were lying in pools of blood, their clothes ripped with bullet holes. Hundreds more wounded people were wandering around in a daze. Others were sitting up, some unable to move, like rabbits in a trap.

The war was done. Like actors in some horror play, the police were leaving the stage, show over, filing back into their *laager*. The Saracen tanks were trundling away like rhinos.

Samuel could barely take it in. He wanted to shut his eyes again. Perhaps the nightmare would go away.

All at once, the air was filled with the sirens of ambulances racing to and from the square outside the church. Almost as quickly as they'd fallen, the bodies were being collected up and rushed to the nearest black hospital.

When the hullabaloo had died down, uneasy thoughts started hammering in Sam's brain. What now? How would they live? *Where* would they live? Who was left alive?

In his bones he felt sure his father was dead: that half-surprised, half-hateful look on his face would remain with Sam for ever. But his mother? Little Sally? The last he remembered was his mother pitching forward on her face and lying still, her skirt all rucked up, showing patchy brown legs. Sally had fallen almost at once across his mother, a jagged line of red holes in the back of her light blue frock.

Unable to take it in at the time, he recalled thinking

how cross his mother would be about the spoiled frock; she'd have to wash and mend it all over again. Sally ought to have been more careful. . .

Perhaps his mother and sister were just wounded. Perhaps they'd fainted. Hardly surprising, really, given the pandemonium. With any luck, an ambulance had whisked them off to hospital. They could be sitting up in bed at this very moment, chatting to a nurse, waiting for a visit.

It was all too much for him. He needed to find his brothers amid the brimming congregation in the church. They'd know what to do.

As he got up on his feet, the doors burst open again and a stocky white man blocked the doorway. He was immaculate in neatly-ironed khaki shirt and shorts, with a peaked cap on his head and a shiny brown leather belt across his chest. On his right hip he wore a black holster.

Even for a white man, his face was uncommonly pale, like a Sunday shirt: washed, starched and ironed. 'Whiter than a pig's underbelly,' as Samuel's mother used to say.

'Leesen ca-a-rrr-refully!' the officer shouted.

He waited until the moans and groans and coughs had died away.

'Leeess-enn!'

His voice echoed eerily round the stone walls, in and out of the oak pews, up to the wooden rafters and down again to the red-tiled floor.

'I . . . am . . . Head of Rand Security. You . . . will . . . obey . . . my . . . orders. . .'

He cut the air with his swagger stick like a cowherd driving cattle to market. Clearing his throat, he spoke huskily and in short bursts, like a machine gun: *rat-ta-tat-tat, rat-ta-tat-tat.*

'Been a riot. . . Troublemakers . . . got their desserts . . . Bystanders accidentally hurt. . . All the mob's fault. . .'

He didn't seem to believe his own words. The evidence of his own eyes must have told him differently. But, after another wave of his stick, he gave out orders – in a single gulp.

While he was speaking, Samuel heard the grinding and screeching of trucks and ambulances drawing up outside the church. A group of stretcher-bearers came rushing through the doors, but were brusquely waved aside until the security man had spelled out his commands.

'Form up in ranks! Those in need of hospital treatment – to the left. Walking wounded – to the right. Come on, move! Urgent cases only!' The last sentence was directed at the ambulance men.

Amid the deathly hush, a tall, thin, bearded white man in black robes came walking slowly down the aisle towards the policeman, his black shoes clip-clopping over the tiles. He was clutching a bible to his chest like a shield.

'My son,' he said, looking the cocked gun in the eye, 'I think you should leave the house of God.'

For a full minute, the two men stared at each other, the one with the gun, the other with the bible.

The bible won. Abruptly, the police officer turned on his heel and marched through the open doors.

'Phew! That was a close shave,' remarked a boy sitting on a pew.

'White to white, too,' muttered his neighbour. 'Lucky the vicar's not black.'

The churchman's voice rang hollowly through the church. It had lost its bravado.

'My children, better do as he says. Walking wounded to the front, beside the font. The rest, stay where you are for the moment.'

The crowd sheltering in the church started dividing up – some limping, shuffling, stumbling towards the stone font. The others remained sitting or lying on pews and floor, unable to shuffle off anywhere except to the grave. Amidst the straggly bunch Samuel suddenly caught sight of Looksmart, a streaky pink rag over one ear.

Thank God!

As Sam ran to join him, Looksmart gave a grim smile.

'Hi, kid. Thank Heavens you're safe and sound. Any sign of Nicky?'

Samuel shrugged. They mounted the altar steps together to get a better view of the church. Nicodemus must have spotted them first, for a bloody hand waved from behind a pew, and an unmistakable husky-squeaky voice called out, 'Over here!'

As their gaze settled on the waving arm, the hidden voice shouted, 'Got a gammy leg.'

Well, at least he was alive. On one leg or two wasn't clear.

'Boy,' said Looksmart – his were deep, hoarse tones, since he was fifteen, and now, possibly, head of the family – 'go and see to your brother. Sneak a ride to hospital and scout around for Mum, Dad and Sally. They could just be wounded. That happens, you know. One bullet knocks you out for a while, then you come to.'

He seemed to be trying to convince himself.

'But they'll see I'm not a stretcher case,' Samuel objected, still uncertain what the police would do with the wounded.

'Oh, they won't bother with a *laetie* like you. If they ask, say you've got internal bleeding – yeah, bleeding cheek!' They both gave a nervous giggle.

Samuel scurried back to the side aisle towards the waving arm, still bowing low as if dodging bullets.

Nicky was lying in a patch of dried blood, one shoe still shiny black, the other dark red and dripping blood. Someone had done their best to stem the flow with a rough tourniquet from a ripped shirt. With one hand, Nicky was squeezing the wound hard, but it was like trying to stop a leaking tap. He needed attention quicky, or he'd bleed to death.

Samuel tore off his T-shirt and wrapped it round the already-bandaged wound. Nicky put one finger on the knot as his brother pulled as tightly as he could.

'Thanks, little'un,' he sighed. 'Christ, it hurts!'

And he shut his eyes.

CHAPTER
FOUR

Samuel and Nicky were carried out to the waiting trucks. They'd drawn the short straw – a bumpy, open truck stinking of rotten cabbages. With a police escort's siren blaring, it raced through the deserted streets, down the road south of Johannesburg towards the hospital.

Above the throaty engine roar and the grinding of the gears, they could hear a radio jabbering away in staccato Afrikaans. The crackling words *Onmiddellik! Onmiddellik!* were repeated over and over again: 'Emergency! Emergency!'

Panic filled the air. It was as if the police realised they'd gone too far and they might have to pay dearly.

And again, at the hospital, the same mad panic. Black orderlies bumped into white nurses, knocking trays and buckets over with a clang. Stretcher-bearers tripped over, tipping casualties onto the floor with

a bump. Doctors ran round muttering, 'No beds. . .
No beds. . .'

The hospital had room for fifty patients, sixty at a
stretch. Now it was faced with several hundred. The
security man from the church took charge. He was
standing in the yard, cane in one hand, gun in
the other.

'Casualty!' he barked above the din. 'Fill the
casualty wards first. Two to a bed, top to tail. Aisles!
Corridors! Not enough beds? Stack them on stretcher
racks. When they're full, dump the bodies on the
floor, idiots!'

Despite doctors' pleas, he roared out, 'No, no, no,
man! No blacks to white or coloured hospitals. They
stay right here. D'ya hear?'

As the stretcher cases waited their turn for
unloading, they watched the policeman strut about
the yard, wiping his sweaty brow with a freckled
hand, yelling orders in English and Afrikaans, hitting
out at orderlies who got in his way.

'Make space on the verandahs, man! Fresh air
won't kill them. What? All full? Right, lay them out
in the grounds. Sun, air and water,' (it had started
to rain) '– best doctors for blacks!'

Samuel heard him shout to another white

policeman, 'We should shoot all these bloody *kaffirs* dead – then they'd behave themselves!'

Samuel searched everywhere for his parents and little Sally. Under trees and bushes, in wards, corridors and stretcher racks, on verandahs, operating tables, even stone slabs in the hospital morgue. He was beginning to think the worst.

He saw sights no child should ever see: bloody stumps of arms and legs, open stomachs spilling out pink chitterlings, knives burrowing into naked chests, saws chewing through flesh and bone.

He heard sounds no youngster should ever hear: the screaming of girls and boys on operating tables with no drugs to dull the pain, the uncontrollable sobbing of young nurses, the crazed shrieks of little children seeing their own blood gushing out, the sound of silence from a grieving mother.

Samuel watched Nicky under the surgeon's knife. Though he held his brother's hand tightly, Nicky couldn't help yelling as the scalpel dug out a .303 bullet from his thigh. Samuel rescued both the bullet and his own bloodied shirt from the swab bin. Nobody cared. Who knows, he thought angrily, one day he might give the bullet back to the man who'd given it to Nicky!

Fortunately for Nicky, his cries of pain blocked out the surgeon's hurried consultation with his assistant: remove the leg or not? A shrill 'No!' from Sam made the 'knife-man' waver. Looking down at the young boy, he smiled wearily, shrugged and sighed.

'OK, Sunny Jim. But if he conks out, you've only yourself to blame.'

He dressed the wound with a lint pad and clean bandage. Then he waved a tired hand at the waiting orderlies to take Nicky away.

'Next!'

Samuel felt violently sick. Only his duty to Nicky kept him from throwing up on the sea-green lino.

Holding one hand over his mouth, he tagged along behind his brother's stretcher. One thought ticked away in his confused mind: today he had good cause to hate all whites. Yet the surgeon was white, and he obviously cared for his patients – all of them black. He was doing everything he could to ease their pain and save lives. Whether the colour of their skin mattered to him, Samuel didn't know. But one thing was clear: *not all whites were evil.*

Once Nicky was tucked up in a grey blanket and left in a corner of the ward, Samuel took his chance to scout for the rest of his family. Although he'd scoured the inner rooms and wards of the hospital, he hadn't yet searched the grounds. He needed to make haste while it was still light.

It was as he came racing round the corner of the ambulance park that he ran full tilt into a brick wall. Or so it seemed. Bouncing off, he collapsed in a heap upon the ground. Dazed, he looked up. A man steadily took shape, like a genie from a bottle.

The man was as startled as the young boy. He had the look of an ox charged by a runt piglet.

'*Opstaan, stront!* (Stand up, little shit!),' he cried.

With one strong hand he yanked the boy up and began to poke his bare chest with a gun. Then, all at once, he did something unexpected. He threw back his head and laughed – a rasping cackle.

'*Ag, so!* A kaffir piccaninny! What are you doing?'

With all the breath knocked out of him, Samuel could only gasp, 'Nothing, sir.'

'*Nothing, sir!*' mimicked the officer in a high-pitched whine. 'Are you wounded?'

'No, sir.'

'What are you doing here, then?'

Sam explained as best he could about his family.

'*Voetsek!* Get the hell out of here before I put a bullet through you!' the officer bellowed.

Signalling with his gun, he summoned a black constable.

'Interrogate this *impimpi* spy at the station. Check his family's passbooks. Get going!'

CHAPTER FIVE

Two policemen frogmarched the boy through the hospital gates and threw him into the back of their riot car. Samuel cowered on the floor as the jeep bumped and crunched over dirt tracks for some forty minutes.

At the police station all was quiet, apart from a new noise that set Samuel's nerves on edge – the howling of police dogs. Like every other black child, Sam believed that police dogs were wolves trained for the police force. He wondered if he was to be thrown to the wolfhounds. As he shrank into a corner, the two black constables sat down at a bare table and stared at him. There was no pity showing in their eyes, no sympathy for a fellow black.

'*Umlungu* (the white man) says we're to question you,' said the fat one, puffing out his chest and lips as if addressing a grown-up thug. 'Did you take part in the riot?'

'No, *nkosi*,' Samuel whined, in imitation of his father whenever he had to show his pass.

'Did you throw stones?' asked the other, a beanpole of a man.

'No, *nkosi*.'

'Where do you live?'

Sam chanted his address as if it were the first lines of the Lord's Prayer.

'Who's the head of your family?'

'My father, *nkosi*.'

The interrogation was getting tiresome for the policeman.

'What does he do?'

He told them, adding, 'I think he's dead. My mother, too.'

'Could you identify them?'

For a moment the boy thought he would have to pick them out of an identity parade.

'Yes, *nkosi*,' he said, confused.

'Come.'

The fat policeman stood up. Dumbly, Samuel followed him down a low passageway dimly lit by paraffin lamps. On both sides there were pressed steel doors with a spy-hole and wooden shutter at the top. The dingy corridor stank of rat droppings. At the far end the officer halted, took a huge, jangling bunch of keys from his belt and unlocked the steel door. With one hand he struck a match and lit the paraffin lamp inside.

As the steel door creaked open, the smell hit Sam full in the face. It was a mixture of stale sweat and boiled cabbage, with some undefinable rotten stench.

He turned quickly away, holding a hand over his nose and mouth, trying to keep from retching.

No attempt had been made to set out the bodies in rows or stacks. They lay where they'd been tossed like so many sacks of potatoes, piled one on top of the other. Lifeless arms and legs sprawled over sightless faces.

'Look, man! Or you'll taste my *sjambok*!'

The black policeman squeezed Sam's head in both hands and twisted it round so that he faced the open cell. Samuel kept his eyes tightly shut. A blow from behind made his eyeballs almost pop out of their sockets. He couldn't help himself: his eyes opened wide, staring, searching.

Three colours flashed before him: blue, black, orange.

A pale blue frock.

A faded black suit.

An orange headscarf.

That was enough. Some gibberish fell from his lips.

'What?' Another blow, this time on his shoulders.

More unconnected words. 'Oh, no, Mum . . . Sally. . . '

Beanpole yelled to his partner, 'Peter, come here, man. Bring some labels.'

Beanpole's large hand encircled the boy's head, holding it in a vice-like grip so that he faced forward. Samuel's eyes and fists were screwed tight. The fat man waddled down the passageway with a fistful of buff labels and a ball of string. When he reached the cell, Beanpole barked, 'Which, boy?'

With a trembling finger, Samuel pointed to the blue, orange and black.

'Sister. Mother. Father.'

'Names!' yelled the fat man, pencil and labels ready.

'Sally – girl. Victoria – mother. Albert – father. Family name Gqibela.'

The officer bent to tie the label to a wrist or an ankle.

'Right, boy,' said Beanpole, straightening up, 'get down to the township board with your birth certificate first thing tomorrow. Now – *voetsek!*

And keep your mouth sealed or you'll be joining the stiffs!'

Samuel needed no second bidding. Running back down the corridor, he dashed through the office and out of the iron gates before they let loose the wolfhounds. He didn't stop running until he reached home.

Home Sweet Home. Even if it was a shabby shack clothed in darkness. Here, at least, he was safe. But where was Looksmart? He sat on his parents' bed, his head in his hands. All the pent-up pain and suffering of the worst day of his life now came gushing out.

When he woke up next morning, Sam's first thought was that the nightmare had gone in the night. Yet the silence in the shack was a sinister reminder of reality. No sleepy yells, no breakfast *pap 'n vleis* – porridge and meat – smells, no hustle and bustle in and out to the 'long drop', as they called it, to empty the chamber pot. It was like dawn breaking over a battlefield.

Samuel felt lonely and scared. Where was Looky?

No sooner had his brain asked the question, than the door swung open and in walked his brother. Sam could tell from Looky's face that he knew.

'How's Nicky?' were his first words.

'OK. He's being taken care of.'

'How long will they keep him in?'

'Dunno. Few days, I reckon.'

Looksmart was obviously reluctant to say the inevitable. At last, he muttered, 'They kept us in all night, then took us to the police station at first light – to identify the bodies.'

'Yes, I know.' Tears started in Samuel's eyes.

Once more the house went quiet, a silence broken only by Sam's snivels and Looksmart's heavy breathing. The older boy was pacing up and down like a caged lion, head bowed, hands clutching his head. Finally he spat out, 'They think that because they've got guns and tanks, they can do what they bloody well like. Well, whitey, your time is up. *Our* time is coming. Blacky isn't going to lie down and take it any more!'

It was a while before Looksmart had walked the fury out of himself. Clearing his throat, he finally sat down on the bed; when he spoke, his words came out quiet and unsure. Then they picked up speed.

'We're on our own now. We've no money for rent or food. We haven't a passbook between us – and you know what that means. We'll have to quit school and get jobs. Otherwise we'll be in deep shit with the police. We have to go and register.'

At midday, the two brothers walked to the other end of the township, to the Advisory Board on Third Avenue. Even from a distance they could see the queue winding round the wide, dusty courtyard, out along the high barbed-wire fence. Many were women with babies strapped to their backs. Others were men sullenly waiting to get their passes stamped for work in the gold mines. The brothers tagged on the back.

Four hours later, they were ushered into a narrow waiting room by a black official.

'Wait till you're called,' he ordered. 'The *Baas* is having his tea break.'

Half an hour later he returned, beckoning to them. They walked nervously down a dark corridor behind the clerk. The man stopped before a glass door and knocked politely. At a sound from within, he pushed open the door and led the pair into a well-lit office smelling richly of cigar smoke.

Seated at a desk was an elderly white man with a white military moustache tinged with yellow. He was peering over the top of his half-moon spectacles at some papers. His thin, pale lips were curled about a thick cigar which kept flashing red, like robot lights.

Without glancing up, he said, 'John here informs me you want to register for a pass. I take it these are your parents' papers?'

'Yes, sir,' said Looksmart meekly. 'They died in the shooting.'

'Troublemakers, eh?'

'Beg pardon, sir?' said Looksmart.

'Your parents were shot while rioting.'

'No, sir!' objected Looksmart hotly. 'They wouldn't do that. They were just bystanders.'

The superintendent's face turned from rose-pink to blood-red.

'Don't come in here blathering, boy. Only criminals were shot yesterday – do you hear?'

Looksmart bit his tongue.

Turning to the black official by the door, the superientendent called out, 'John, bring me the man's file. Hurry, boy!'

The man jumped like a startled rabbit and pulled open a filing cabinet drawer.

'Which heading, *baas*?'

'Male, Pass Control.'

'Coming, *mei baas*,' whined the man, pulling a file out of the drawer. He trotted over to the desk and placed it before his master.

In silence, the superintendent examined the file, glancing now and then at their parents' passbooks. Suddenly he removed the cigar from his mouth and looked up, flinging a hand in Sam's direction.

'What's that piccaninny doing here?'

'He's my brother,' said Looksmart.

'Is he registered?'

'Yes, sir.'

'Where's his birth certificate, baptism papers?'

'At home, sir. My father was very hot on keeping everything in order.'

'Good.' Bending over a brand new black passbook, the superintendent scribbled some words. Finally, he banged down the stamp so hard that cigar ash scattered all over the desk.

'There you are, boy. Now you're fully equipped to go where you belong – Bantu homelands!'

The two brothers stared in disbelief.

'B-but, I was born here. I go to school here,' stuttered Looksmart.

'Any African who isn't needed for serving white business must go to the tribal reserve. That's the law of the land.'

The man was clearly growing impatient.

'You and your brother are no use to the township.

Here, take your pass and clear off.'

Looksmart took the book in silence, stunned by the man's words. Surely there must be some mistake? They'd never been near any homelands in their lives. To Samuel, the word 'homelands' conjured up scenes from a Tarzan film, but without Tarzan and Jane: jungles full of snakes and killer ants, scorching plains where lions and elephants roamed, fierce tribes and cannibals. But in the land of the white *baas*, all they could do was obey. They were helpless.

'Show them out, John,' snapped the superintendent. 'Next!'

CHAPTER SIX

When they got home, Looksmart fished out an old envelope from what their father called his 'treasure chest' – a battered old cigar box he kept under a brick in the corner. Then he sat down to write a letter to their father's brother, an uncle they knew only by name.

Samuel took the letter to the post office in the Indian quarter with coins for a stamp. Mr Naidoo, the postmaster, weighed the letter, stuck on a stamp and handed back some change. It was like posting a letter to Father Christmas. You never expected it to arrive, let alone to receive a reply.

Yet a reply did come, three weeks later. Mr Naidoo walked all the way to the house to deliver it himself. The letter was brief. In a bold scrawl, it said simply: *Come, my sons. Meet at Mmabatho Station on Friday 2 May, 4 o'clock. Uncle Sabata.*

No ifs and buts. Family clearly meant a lot to their father's brother.

A few days remained to their departure deadline. After telling their landlord, they stuffed all their possessions into two small bundles and sold the rest. Neighbours paid a few rand for the furniture – bed, table, chairs and shelves, pots, pans, iron and bucket. They were left with their two bed mats – the only reminders of their family home.

With some of the money Looky and Sam bought train tickets to Mmabatho, as Uncle Sabata had instructed, and bus tickets to Nicky's hospital at Vereeniging. The day before their departure, they took the bus to see Nicky. He wouldn't know anything about the deaths of their parents, nor of his future exile. If he was fit enough, they could all go together to 'Ma-ma', as they called Mmabatho. The name sounded like some exotic land.

But bad news awaited them at the hospital. Nicky was not fit to go. He had had to have an emergency operation the day before. When they were shown into the ward, he was just coming round from the anaesthetic.

The patients had thinned out since Samuel's last visit. Now, the gardens and verandahs were more or less free of stretchers and beds, though the corridors and wards were filled with the wounded, some two to a bed. Nicky was one of the lucky ones: his was a single bed in a sunny window alcove at the far end of a long ward. There was even a wooden chair beside the iron bed; the two brothers shared it.

The ward sister was a big black woman, hostile to all comers. She was one of those women who have two halves: the upper half was top heavy, but fairly well-proportioned, while the lower half spread out like a saucer round a tea-cup. She didn't so much walk as waddle – two steps sideways, one step forward. Woe betide anything that got in her way: it was swept up like debris. And her bark was as bad as her bulk. She grumbled at them for being too early for visiting hours, for bringing filthy germs into her hospital, for being under-age, for getting in her way.

At last, she hissed, 'Break it to him gently. He doesn't know.'

They both stared round as she moved off, her bulky bottom like two great pistons on some old factory machinery.

Perhaps word had reached the hospital of their family's deaths and their exile. How else could she know?

Nicky looked pinched and leathery. But as far as they could see, all his parts seemed to be in place, if not yet in working order. It took a while for him to get them into focus. He gazed at the unfamiliar sight of his lanky elder brother smartened up for the visit – white shirt, jeans and shiny black shoes. Sitting beside him was his kid brother in T-shirt and *takkies*.

First he seemed to recognise them, then he stared right through them.

'Looky . . . Sammy,' he finally said.

They smiled encouragingly. His next words wiped the smiles off their faces.

'Mum? Dad?'

Looksmart didn't beat about the bush. 'They're dead, Nicky. Sally too. Shot.'

The news brought down the shutters of Nicky's eyes and left his head motionless on the striped grey pillow. Occasionally he gave a start, his head jerking to and fro, his fists clenching and unclenching.

They sat there patiently, waiting for him to return to the land of the living. It was no use telling him about their travel plans if he couldn't take them in. The anaesthetic seemed to be wearing off and his raw nerve ends were jangling about inside him.

All at once, unable to keep silent any longer, Samuel burst out, 'Howd'ya feel, Nicky?'

Looksmart put a finger to his lips and scowled.

They were both startled to hear Nicky's low voice. 'My leg hurts.'

For the first time their attention was drawn to the thin brown blanket. It looked odd. There was a bulge about as long as a chair leg, but only on one side, extending evenly from the middle of the bed nearly to the white bars at the bottom. On the other side, the lump ended in mid-thigh. After that . . . nothing.

They thought that perhaps the bed had a guttering holding the left leg. Other patients had a leg raised in the air, while some had a leg lowered on a shelf.

'Which one, Nick?'

'Left. Pins and needles in my toes.'

Samuel stared from Nicky's covered right foot to the flat blanket where the left foot should be. It was then that the ward sister's words hit him.

They'd cut off his leg.

Looksmart's expression didn't change, but a stern, hard look formed a film over his normally kind, brown eyes. He must be feeling the weight of brotherhood. It was either up to him or the ward sister to break the news.

'Nicky, be brave. You're alive. You'll soon be well and leave hospital. You'll get married, have children, be happy . . . uh . . . but you won't be quite the same.

None of us will. . .'

He cleared his throat for one last effort.

'You've lost a leg, brother. . .' He waited for his word to sink in before adding, 'in the cause of freedom.'

There didn't seem much connection between freedom and a lost leg. But Looksmart hurried on, as if words could smother the anguish of living on one leg. He said anything that came into his head: angry curses against the police and whites, then the whole catalogue of events, ending with the exile order.

'We'll all meet up when you're well,' he said. 'And as soon as we reach Ma-ma, we'll write and tell you all about the cows and goats. Then, when you join us, you'll live on milk and honey, grow fit and strong, and have four beautiful young wives to look after you.'

Before Nicky could say anything, the battleship ward sister came padding up. Her mood softened once she saw they'd broken the news.

'Shoo!' she growled, waving her arms about like windmill sails. 'Time's up. Patient needs rest. Go on, scram!'

They welcomed the opportunity to go. Pressing Nicky's hands, they left him to his thoughts.

At the far end of the ward, Looksmart approached the sister.

'It's kind of you to let us see our brother. Thanks, Sister.'

She grunted, unused to compliments. Then, as if to explain why the doctors had done what they'd done, she muttered the word 'gangrene'. With a shrug of her shoulders, she added, 'It was the leg or his life.'

Looksmart nodded, though he, like Sam, had no idea what gangrene was.

They made their way out of the hospital, relieved to breathe out the hospital smells and breathe in fresh air.

It was to be another five years before Samuel saw Nicky again.

● ● •

Early on the morning of Deadline Day, Samuel and Looksmart set off to walk the two miles to the station. Like a couple of tramps, they carried their worldly possessions on a stick over their shoulders. There was no one to see them off, apart from two yard dogs who trotted beside them to the fringe of town. There they halted. The black mongrels squatted on their haunches, brushing the dust with their tails as if waving goodbye, and watched the boys disappear over the hump of the hill.

The two boys cast a final glance at the township. In the early morning haze, with a streaky orange sky as a backdrop, the great sprawl of lean-tos had an unreal, almost romantic look about it. A wave of melancholy swept over Samuel. This was the only home he'd ever known. Would he ever see it again? Smell its homely smells? Wake up to its cocks crowing?

'Come on, *laetie*,' said Looksmart with a sigh, as they stepped forward to mud huts and leopard-skins, bogeymen and witch doctors.

They trudged on. Into exile. Into the land of Uncle Sabata. Into the land where Africans were supposed to live in peace, governing themselves. Where pink men were as rare as pink elephants. Perhaps it wouldn't be so bad, after all. . .

CHAPTER
SEVEN

Even though it was still early, the railway halt was teeming with workers in dusty dungarees; they were waiting on the opposite side of the platform, taking the train to the factories and mills of nearby Vereeniging and Boipatong. Looksmart and Sam were heading north west, first to Klerksdorp, then on to Mmabatho and Uncle Sabata.

The local steam train was bursting at the seams. Workers were hanging out of windows, lying flat on carriage roofs, clinging to doorposts or the backs of other travellers. There seemed to be more people outside than inside the train. It reminded Samuel of an anthill swarming with insects.

With a hoot and a rumble and grinding of wheels, the train wheezed its way out of the station. It was a miracle how it managed to get up enough steam to pull such a load.

The brothers braced themselves to leap on to their

train and claim whatever foothold they could among the heaving bodies. They were in for a shock. As their train pulled into the halt, they found themselves almost alone on the platform; no one was clinging to the carriage roof or anyone else's coat-tails.

Instead of a smoke-blackened, windowless row of grimy wagons hauled by an old locomotive, the train was a veritable stately home on wheels drawn by a magnificent black-and-red elephant-like engine. The coaches gleamed alternately brown-and-cream, green-and-black, red-and-white – like a cavalcade of expensive limousines.

The guard had yelled 'Klerksdorp' – that was them! As a door opened, Sam scrambled up. In his haste, he blocked the way of passengers trying to get off. Above the clatter and squeal of wheels he could hear the guard shouting something, but he could not make it out.

Once inside the compartment, however, he soon realised his mistake.

It was a white carriage.

The appearance of a black boy so startled the two pink ladies trying to get out that they let out hysterical screams. Their shrieks brought a black guard rushing down the platform, waving a red flag in one hand

and a whistle in the other. He was blowing the whistle for all he was worth.

'*Voetsek, kaffir!*' he yelled. 'Can't you read? *Slegs Blankes* – Whites Only!'

In his eagerness Samuel hadn't seen the sign on the front of the coach. Realising his error, he tried to back off. But he caught his tramp's stick in the doorway and however hard he tugged, he couldn't get it out.

Since he'd never been on a train before, and he'd only seen blacks on trains, it never entered his head that whites also travelled by train. He had always assumed that they all used cars.

Bellowing in his ear, 'I said, get off, *kaffir*!' the guard grabbed Samuel by the scruff of the neck and yanked him off the train, snapping his stick in two. Samuel tumbled backwards. He would have bumped his head on the tarmac, had Looksmart not caught him.

The obstruction removed, the guard hurriedly turned his attention to the distraught ladies.

'Sorry, *mei baas*,' he said in grovelling tones. 'Him make *lo mal* mistake. Him not read. Forgive him, *mei baas*. This *kaffir piccaninny* not know coach for white people.'

Samuel stood by, unable to believe his eyes as

the guard wiped the steps with his white gloves. All the while he bleated, 'Sorry, *mei baas*. Sorry, *mei baas*.'

The two elderly ladies stepped down in as dignified a way as possible, still shocked at seeing a black devil burst into their carriage. As soon as they'd gone, the guard turned to the youngsters. His tone switched abruptly from whine to bark.

'Why'd you get on the wrong coach? Putting the fear of God into decent people? I could have you arrested! Don't they teach you *kaffirs* anything?' He waved his arms to impress any whites watching. 'Are you colour-blind? Can't you tell a white carriage from a black carriage? Get to the back of the train! And remember in future to read the signs: EUROPEANS ONLY. NON-EUROPEANS ONLY. WHITES ONLY. NON-WHITES ONLY. That's what they're there for.'

In the wooden-seated Non-White carriage at the end of the train, the boys squeezed onto a narrow bench opposite an old woman and a smartly-dressed young man. The woman was as black as night; her large bulk took up most of the seat, and her bird-like eyes darted here, there and everywhere, as she chewed her tobacco.

The man in the dark pin-stripe suit was a lighter shade of burnished walnut, slim, smoothly shaven and wearing black-rimmed glasses. He held a thick book on his lap, but was too busy staring at the new passengers to read it for the moment.

Evidently the whole carriage had witnessed the kerfuffle. Samuel didn't know where to put himself. He tried to make himself as small as possible, pressing into Looksmart's shoulder. In the space of a few minutes, he'd experienced Apartheid as never before. He was venturing into the multi-coloured world and seeing what blackness really meant. It was most confusing. Should he feel shame or anger? The large woman's face looked as if she'd just bitten on a maggoty apple – and Samuel was the maggot!

No sooner had the whistle blown and the train lurched forward, than the woman resumed her chewing. Her jaws worked up and down to the rhythm of the train, slowly picking up speed. All at once she stopped, and fixed her beady eyes on the boy.

'You troublemaker?' she squawked.

With the question out, she continued her chewing to the beat of the tracks: *clickety-clack, clickety-clack, clickety-clack.*

Sam blurted out his innocence. 'No, no, I'm not.' He bowed his head.

'You're too young to know the ways of the world,' she continued. She stopped to bite off a new plug of tobacco with a single, long brown tooth.

'We live in our world. Whites live in theirs. We're their servants. They're our masters. See? Whether we like it or not.'

She opened the window and spat out a long stream of browny-black liquid.

But she hadn't finished.

'Blacks and whites live apart. That's how it's always been. That's how it always will be. It's how white people want it. We have to obey, see?'

As she was talking, the man beside her looked uneasy. He removed his glasses and half-turned away. But the word 'obey' stirred him to life.

'Excuse me, Mother,' he said politely. 'It doesn't have to be like this. In the past, maybe. But a new generation of Africans is growing up; they go to school and know enough about the world to ask questions. Some of them aren't prepared to lie down and be trampled on by white boots.'

Samuel looked hard at the softly-spoken man. He was different from workers in the township, and from Coloured clerks and Indian stall-holders.

'We were in the shootings,' Samuel muttered.

The woman grunted. 'That's what I'm saying, sonny. They've got the guns. What can we do against guns?'

'I'm sorry,' said the young man, 'but if you'll pardon me for saying, we must learn a lesson from what happened. It could be a turning-point. Now's the time to start fighting back.'

The woman's chewing changed gear again, before grinding to a halt.

'Oh yeah,' she sneered. 'Attack whites with spears and clubs! It's rabble-rousers like you who get innocent children killed.'

'You're right, Mother,' he said calmly. 'We must avoid bloodshed if we can. But we have to defend ourselves. We can get guns from our friends outside the country. And we can form commando units to raid white munition dumps. But without guns, we have no way of defending ourselves.'

Looksmart's eyes shone. More than his brother, he was excited by what the man was saying. Just then, however, the black ticket inspector came down the centre corridor; he was accompanied by a short, sandy-haired police officer smoking a cigarette. For one awful moment, Sam thought they'd come to arrest him.

'Tickets and passes!' shouted the inspector.

The old woman bent down to rummage noisily in the canvas bag beneath her feet, while her neighbour put a hand into an inside pocket. Looksmart had his paper and tickets handy.

'Are you for Klerksdorp?' The policeman's question was addressed to all three, but it was the woman who hastened to reply.

'I'm going to see my son, *mei baas*. He works there. Him good boy.'

'Are you sure?' said the white man, raising his voice. He was obviously enjoying his power over the frightened woman.

'Oh yes, yes, *mei baas, mei makulu baas. Mini makulu* sure. He garden boy for *makulu* white family. He always keep nose clean, *mei baas.*'

Tired of her cringing, the officer puffed smoke in her face, before turning to the others. Examining the brothers' papers, he gave a contemptuous sneer.

'Back to where you belong.'

Turning to the last passenger, the guard said, 'You, boy, show me your pass.'

Slowly the black man stood up, brushed the creases from his suit and adjusted his glasses. As he thrust his documents under the policeman's nose, he said clearly and precisely, 'As you see, sir, I am a full head taller than you.'

The officer's hand flew to his gun holster, thinking he was about to be assaulted. But, seeing the calm face staring down at him, he relaxed.

'What's your point, boy?' he demanded.

'Well, if I'm a boy, what are you?'

The white man pulled himself up to his full height, bringing his nose up to the young man's chest. With a superior smile, he said, 'The difference between us, *boy*, is obvious. *I* have the gun and *you* haven't.'

The black man glanced meaningfully at Samuel and Looksmart before replying, 'Right you are, sir.'

Handing back the documents, the policeman moved on with the ticket inspector in tow. He didn't hear the low murmur behind him: 'For the moment, *mei baas*. Just for the moment.'

● ● ●

The remainder of the journey passed without interruption. The young man was from a black law firm in Johannesburg. He was on his way to advise a black client under house arrest near Klerksdorp.

Taking off his glasses, he leant forward and said earnestly, 'My young friends, I would say this to you: seize every bit of education you can.'

But what education did the boys need for herding goats?

CHAPTER
EIGHT

The nearer the train came to Mmabatho, the lighter was the load. The stout woman and the lawyer both got off at Klerksdorp, and nearly all the white passengers had disappeared at country stations and halts along the way.

The brothers watched them go. For the most part, judging by their quaint clothing, the whites were farming families. The men were bearded and wore corduroy trousers, flowery waistcoats, heavy jackets and long boots. The women were in white bonnets and flowing black cloaks. Strange clothes, strange people under an African sun.

The farms they passed lay snug in the folds of low, rolling hills surrounded by tall feather grass. Here and there, the wild expanses had been fenced off into rich pastures for herds of well-padded cattle. Tumbling streams, catching the rays of the sun, glinted like silver ribbons running through the valleys. Along the banks hung cascading weeping willows and lemon trees. Sometimes, in the distance, they spotted a horse-drawn cart, kicking up dust clouds as it clattered from farm to hamlet.

Looksmart had fallen asleep, but Samuel was too enthralled by the view through the window to close his eyes.

Some of the smaller homesteads were surrounded by native *marula* and mango trees, pawpaws and papaya growing wild, and tall banana palms. The bigger farms were approached through long avenues of jacarandas trumpeting their brilliant, lavender-blue blooms.

Not all the farms were so prosperous. Alongside the railway track, catching the fertile soot, were small-holdings with whitewashed cottages housing the noisy families of poor white farmers. Sometimes their little children would tumble out of doors to wave at the lucky passengers. And Sam would wave and smile back at children who did not distinguish black from white.

It was good farming soil, fertile and well-watered. A green and pleasant land. So this was the *real* South Africa, the land some called 'Paradise on Earth'.

Reading his thoughts, Looksmart, who was now

fully awake, muttered, 'Just think of the tribes that once inhabited these grassy plains! Their blood and bones are feeding the soil. No wonder the earth is so red!'

As the train chugged into Mafeking, a distinct change came over the land. It was as if they'd reached the end of a giant carpet that ran into the foothills. Here, on the other side of the ridge, the land was yellow and brown, flat and treeless, with just the occasional clump of poplars huddled together like lean and hungry men against the wind.

'Next stop . . . Mmabatho!' shouted the guard. 'Ter-min-usss!'

End of the line. End of South Africa. Samuel imagined falling off a cliff at the country's end, tumbling into the ocean or some deep abyss. Of course, he'd heard of far-off England and Holland where the Europeans came from. But his young brain somehow fancied that those crusts of land had crumbled into the sea, forcing people to sail away in ships to Africa.

Seeing Sam's puzzled frown, Looksmart explained, 'We're close to the border now. Botswana's the next country. Even if we Africans were permitted to leave the country, we wouldn't want to go to Botswana.

It's mainly desert – the Kalahari.'

'Oh, my.' So that explained the dry, corn-coloured landscape beyond the window, and the reddish dust swirling about trying to uproot the wiry shrubs that clung doggedly to the sandy soil.

Sam stared uneasily at the shifting sands, wondering how anyone could live in such a place. But he didn't have long to feed his imagination, for the train was approaching its final stop. Being a frontier post, Mmabatha was more of a fortress than a town, with jeeps and *bakkies* stirring up billowing clouds of dust on the tracks running alongside the railway line.

The station was full of soldiers. Goodness knows what they were doing there. Stopping Africans from getting out or getting in? Or perhaps they were there to keep hungry lions out. Mind you, what animal in its right mind would want to come to the land of Apartheid? *Black rhinos to the left, white rhinos to the right. Coloured giraffes down the centre lane, if you please!*

As the brothers walked down the platform, they had no idea who was meeting them. Surely they were easy enough to spot? After wandering round the station, they emerged into the sunshine of the one and only street, and looked hopefully in both directions.

While they were standing by the roadside, they heard the most appalling racket – a clanking, burping, rumbling and *phut-phutting*. Looking towards the noise, they saw, coming towards them, a huge, black Rolls Royce.

It was not a smooth-running, sleek limousine. The car coughed and sneezed its way forward in fits and starts. To their amazement, the contraption pulled up at the kerb right beside them. The driver's door swung open and out stepped the strangest figure they'd ever set eyes on.

He was a thick-set African wearing a stove-pipe hat, high starched collar and tie, long black tails and striped grey trousers. On his feet were shiny black shoes trimmed with grey spats. He was smoking a Sherlock Holmes pipe, puffing clouds of blue smoke from both corners of his mouth. In one hand he held a fly whisk, which he kept flicking towards them; with the other he leaned on an ebony stick topped by a swan's head.

The boys thought he must be some kind of high-ranking tribal chief or king.

'*Bayete-a-a-a!*' the man cried in a guttural voice.

Was this Uncle Sabata?

Taking the pipe from his mouth, the man grinned from ear to ear, and said in English, 'Welcome, my boys, dear old chaps. Jolly good to see you! Come along.'

With a wave of his fly whisk he indicated the waiting limousine.

Was *this* Dad's brother?

They took their places on the cracked, silver-grey leather seat at the back, their bundles across their knees. Despite the soft seats, it was a jolting, bone-shaking, hair-raising journey with Uncle Sabata at the wheel. Once outside the town, they travelled for mile upon mile over dirt tracks and potholes, across a blood-red savannah with not a house or farm in sight. Only when they'd passed a broken post marked BANTU HOMELAND did they start to see signs of life – villages of beehive-shaped mud huts, each with a conical straw roof held up by a wooden pole. Smoke curled up from a hole in the top, escaping into the air. The huts had no windows, just a doorway so low that people had to stoop to pass through it.

Barefoot boys and girls rushed out, hopping up and down, shouting greetings as the motor car swept by. Women stood at the trackside smiling and waving.

Both the women and the children were wearing a single blanket dyed in shades of ochre – from pale brown-yellow to rusty red. Some of the women were hauling pails of water from the well.

They saw no men apart from a few toothless old-timers sitting in the shade of gum trees. When Looksmart questioned Uncle Sabata about it, he grunted, 'My men work in the Reef gold mines. They come back twice a year to plough the fields and scatter the good seed.' He turned and winked meaningfully.

The boys were surprised. So wives and children only saw their menfolk twice a year.

In the bigger villages they passed small primary schools – rough, brick-built, with corrugated roofs. They were only recognisable as schools by the large white boards outside that spelled out BANTU PRIMARY SCHOOL. Every one was deserted. Perhaps it was the holidays – or, more likely, the buildings were just for show, and no one in the villages could read or write.

Late in the afternoon, the motor car drove down a dip in the track and, as it came up the other side, they saw another village in the distance. Without a word, drawing on his pipe, Uncle Sabata pointed imperiously ahead, as if to say, 'We're home.'

Sam counted ten round houses, each washed in white lime and surrounded by colourful gardens at the front, side and rear. Peach and pear trees stood around them, and inside the white garden fences neat rows of marigolds grew around carefully tended lawns.

The brothers watched in awe as Uncle Sabata pulled up before the largest of the houses. He hooted long and loudly and, from out of nowhere, twelve men in faded Western suits appeared. They doffed their homburg hats, bowed low and shouted in chorus, 'All Hail the Chief!'

Uncle Sabata solemnly stepped from the car, stretched lazily and flicked the ash from his suit. Then he re-lit his pipe, puffed a few times and gazed haughtily about him. Like a commander inspecting a guard of honour, he advanced down the line of men, addressing them as his *amaphakathi* or counsellors.

So this was their new father, guardian and mentor, their *tatamkhulu!* They were in luck. Their father had had the good sense to choose an older brother who towered high above other mortals, who was ruler of the entire tribal reserve and master of all he surveyed – as far as the horizon.

What they soon realised, however, was that Uncle

Sabata's land had been granted to him by whites who had no use for it. They'd thrown in the old Rolls and the top hat and tails – which looked suspiciously like an undertaker's cast-offs..

Uncle Sabata later explained that as a boy, he had been educated at mission school and won a rare scholarship to Oxford University in England. But the boys soon saw that he played the English gentleman only when it suited him. In each of the ten round houses or *rondavels* was a wife and children – whom he treated as one big family. Now Looksmart and his brother were to be part of that family.

Uncle Sabata led his older nephew to one of the rondavels, bending low to pass into the dingy interior. Then he took Samuel to another in which, along the clay and wattle walls, the boy counted a dozen bed-rolls neatly stacked on the hard, straw-covered floor.

Aunt Priscilla was there to meet Sam: a large, fierce-looking woman who kept her gaze lowered in her husband's presence. She didn't as much as glance at the boy.

'May I present you with a new son,' announced the Chief in a booming voice. 'Teach him well.'

With that, he was gone, leaving Samuel alone with his new, leathery-faced mother. Yet, in an instant, the ogress turned into a merry sprite with twinkling eyes and a mouthful of big, sparkling teeth. As she rocked to and fro, she spread her arms wide.

'Come, sonny boy. Welcome.'

He sank into her soft embrace and, when he came up for air, she said, with a giggle, 'Don't mind old bossy-boots. We have three rules: work hard, respect the spirits and obey the Chief. Do that, and you'll get along fine. Now, let me explain your chores.

'Boys do the hunting here – for rabbit, bushpig, springbok and ostrich. They kill pests like jackals, foxes and prairie rats, and protect the home from spiders, snakes and scorpions.'

'What do girls do?' Sam asked.

Aunt Priscilla put a finger to her lips.

'Asking questions is a town habit. We don't waste time wagging our tongues; we use our eyes and ears and noses. That's how we learn. But I'll tell you this once. Girls do girls' jobs: milking goats and cows, working with their mothers in the fields – hoeing, planting, watering, grubbing, feeding the chickens, pounding corn.'

By the time Aunt Priscilla had shown Sam round, dusk was falling and his new brothers and sisters were coming home. When all nine boys and girls were present and correct, Aunt Priscilla introduced him.

'This is your new brother.'

Sure enough, no one asked questions, though he noticed a few curious glances, especially from the girls. He had a bed space on the floor between eleven-year-old Jacob and thirteen-year-old Gideon. It was the older boy who taught him all about the household spirits and what had to be done to combat evil. In a hushed voice Gideon explained: 'If you hear strange noises on the rooftop at night, that's the *baloye* – they ride naked on the backs of baboons and if you don't take care, they drink your blood while you're asleep.'

'Oh my!' he exclaimed.

'Then there are the *thickoloshes*. They're small, hairy beasts with faces all squashed up like baboons, and they have long tails.'

Gideon put a hand over his mouth, and said in a whisper, 'They've also got long willies which they carry over their shoulders.'

'Oh my!' Sam said again.

'Only our Chief can talk to the ancestral spirits,' continued Gideon. 'They help us outdo the evil spirits and monsters. He is the *sangoma*, our medicine man.'

The new boy asked no more questions. But that night he watched his new family bury the liver and heart of a goat outside the door. The juicy offerings had vanished by morning, and Gideon smiled happily.

'See – the spirits are grateful for our gifts.'

CHAPTER
NINE

It wasn't long before Looksmart made his escape from the village – with Uncle Sabata's help. At sixteen, a boy became a man overnight. . . and life took an abrupt change of direction.

For every able-bodied man sent to work in the Crown Mines, Uncle Sabata, like other tribal chiefs, received a bounty of cash or gold. So within a month of his arrival, Looksmart was back on the train heading for the great ridge of hills overlooking the Golden City of Johannesburg. There he was promised an office job in Crown Mine No. 3. Since Looksmart could read and write, a rare commodity in the gold mines, he would take a clerical post, the most respected job for a black man in the entire mine.

So Looksmart would now have a decent job, the headman would get an educated employee on low pay, and Uncle Sabata would take his usual cut. Samuel was envious of his brother. Gold had a great glamour about it. He imagined gold mines to be grand open galleries shining and gleaming in the sunshine. Next to them would be vast golden palaces with towers that reached up to the sun. The miners would live in spacious apartments spread across the hillside, so that they could breathe fresh air and spend their spare time and wages in the great city.

He could not have been more wrong.

● ● ●

Time passed. Although Samuel longed to further his education, Uncle Sabata kept all his family and tribespeople away from books. For the time being, the boy's school was the veld, his classmates sheep and goats.

Sam soon came to realise that schooling and education are two different things. Education came from the sights, sounds and smells of the countryside where he worked as a shepherd. He learned to gather wild honey from bees' nests in the hollows of trees, to find the sweet berries and roots you can eat without falling sick, to drink warm, creamy milk straight from a ewe's udder, to swim naked in fresh, clear streams and to catch fish with twine and sharp bits of wire.

And, of course, to steer clear of puff-adders and the deadly mamba.

He came to love the great open spaces of the veld; they went on for ever to the distant, clear horizon. Mother Nature was a great teacher. So was village life. Unlike their life back at the township, here they were all one big family. The children of Uncle Sabata's wives were *his* brothers and sisters; each wife was *his* mother. And Uncle Sabata was *his* father – though, because of his 'royal' status, the family called him *Tatamkhulu*.

Uncle Sabata was a fitness fanatic. Each morning at the crack of dawn he would lead the boys on a run into the veld. Like the others, Samuel would run barefoot over the hard, sandy soil. He was assigned to the second, younger group of boys led by Gideon. By the time he was twelve, however, he had abandoned the younger group and often kept pace with his uncle. But he never dared overtake the Chief; instead, he kept a respectable distance behind him.

Samuel was running well. He knew that he could outpace anyone if he wanted. While his uncle was short of wind, puffing like an old steam-train at the township station, the boy felt as if he were flying on wings. He began to think about his body as a blacksmith's forge. His heart pumped blood to toes and head, like flames to the blazing fire; his lungs blew air like the smith's bellows; his feet beat the ground like a hammer on the anvil. Sometimes he felt he could run for ever, faster than the wind, further than the sun's journey through the sky.

After a rub-down in the stream that ran by the village, Samuel would eat breakfast before jogging the five miles to his flock of goats and sheep. If he spotted a hyena or prairie dog sniffing around his animals he would give chase, sometimes even running the predator down. He loved running in the wild, scaring snakes and scorpions out of his way. Whooping and whistling, he would chase small deer and kudu. In the veld he was utterly alone, with no other human for miles.

But one day he almost paid dearly for his daring. On his return one evening, he spied a herd of grazing buffalo – big black beasts with sharp, gnarled horns on their broad brows. Thinking to have some fun, he ran swiftly through the herd, teasing and scaring them.

But he grew too cocky, tripped over a small rock and went tumbling to the ground. As he tried to jump up, he felt a sharp pain in his right ankle; he couldn't put any weight on it.

Several buffalo lowered their heads and came lumbering towards the wounded animal they saw limping towards a rock wall some hundred paces away.

Each step was sheer torment. He could hear a tearing noise, like cloth ripping, in his damaged ankle. Could he make it to the rocks? Even if he did, how would they save him? He'd be pinned against the wall, with nowhere to run to.

Suddenly the crowding buffalo halted, pawing the ground. For an instant, Samuel thought they'd decided to leave him alone. But no. The circling beasts parted, leaving space for the herd leader to come charging through and deal with the intruder. In that brief moment of hesitation, he staggered to the rock and to his relief found a narrow crack just wide enough for his skinny body to squeeze into.

Never had he prayed so hard to the spirits. Whether they heard him or not, he never discovered. Perhaps they half-heard him, because the massive buffalo could not get at him with its horns or hoofs. All it could do was stick out its slavering tongue and lick his face – hot, sticky, as rough as a thorn bush. His face was soon dripping wet with white slime. He could smell the beast's stinking breath and see its wild black eyes just a few inches from his own.

It seemed an age before the buffalo gave a despairing bellow and backed off. At a distance of several yards it found a more accessible snack of prairie grass, while keeping one baleful eye on the shepherd.

All night long the frightened boy cowered in his hiding-place, unable to evade the buffalo sentries watching him.

At dawn, his heart pounded as he caught the sound of shouts across the plain.

'Here! Over here!!' he shouted as loudly as he could.

It wasn't long before the search party found him and scattered the buffalo herd. He was carried back to the village where Aunt Priscilla wrapped his twisted ankle in soothing herbs and put him to bed.

● ● ●

While Sam was convalescing, Uncle Sabata paid him a visit. To Samuel's surprise, the Chief complimented him.

'Boy, you've got what it takes to run a long distance. Who knows? Maybe you could run a marathon.'

'Thank you, *Tatamkhulu*. What's a marathon?'

The Chief was eager to impart his knowledge. He bent forward and said, 'Listen, I'll tell you a story. It's about a tribe called the Greeks who lived a long time ago. They used to play games to celebrate big occasions like war victories and funerals of great men. Not just running, but wrestling, boxing and chariot-racing too. . .

'They called the games the Olympics, because their favourite arena was at the foot of Mount Olympus – their gods lived at the top. Priests, athletes and spectators came together once every four years, and during the Games, all wars stopped. That's how much they revered the Games.'

Samuel couldn't help himself.

'Did they run a marathon?'

Uncle Sabata shook his head.

'Not in the old days. But when the first modern Olympic Games were held in Athens, the organisers added the marathon in memory of a Greek messenger. Some say he ran twenty-six miles from the port of Marathon to Athens to warn of a Persian attack.'

Samuel was entranced by the story. He imagined running all that way himself.

'Please tell me more, *Tatamkhulu*.'

Uncle Sabata lit his pipe, fell silent for a time, gazing at his nephew's shining eyes. Then, taking the pipe from his mouth, he opened a book he had brought along from his library shelf.

CHAPTER TEN

'I must refresh myself with the names,' he said. 'Ah, yes, here we are.'

He sat down with the open book upon his lap, put on his glasses and began to read, occasionally looking up to add comments of his own.

'In 1896, just seventeen runners gathered at Marathon to run the race – thirteen Greeks, four foreigners, all famous athletes: Teddy Flack from Australia, Arthur Blake of the USA, Albin Lemusiaux of France and Gyula Kellner of Hungary. The favourite, Flack, had already won two gold medals and that same morning had gained a bronze medal for tennis!

'In the afternoon sunshine, at precisely two o'clock, the starter's pistol began the race. The seventeen runners crossed a wide plain, passing through a number of villages, and were cheered on by farmers. . .'

'Who won? Who won?' shouted Samuel, punching the air.

'Not so fast,' said his uncle sternly. 'The marathon is a long race, so my story is long too. Now, let me see. By halfway, the four foreigners were well in the lead, without a home runner in sight. The Frenchman was two miles ahead of the rest. But at twenty miles he was beginning to feel the strain. His lead was down to just one minute and Flack was steadily overhauling him. Behind him came two Greeks: Vasilakos was seven minutes behind, and Spiridon Louis another thirty seconds.'

The boy cheered. 'Come on, Greeks!' he cried. But his uncle was about to dash his hopes.

'The Frenchman was now paying the price for going too fast, too early. Halfway up a hill, he suddenly stopped for a rest. Meanwhile, Flack ran past him, seemingly on the way to his third gold medal. With only three miles to go, Teddy Flack was entering the outskirts of Athens. Not far now. But . . . Flack was slowing down. The Greek Vasilakos was coming into sight.'

That cheered up Samuel. 'Come on, Vassy!' he cried, unable to control himself.

'However. . .' said his uncle with a smile, 'poor Vasilakos was weaving drunkenly from one side of the road to the other. It wasn't long before another

Greek caught up with him: Spiridon Louis. For a while they ran together, before Vasilakos had to drop back, leaving Louis to chase the leader. With only two miles to go, the tall, thin figure of Louis was hot on Flack's heels. But he was desperately tired. So tired, that he was on the point of dropping out, when he heard a familiar voice. His girlfriend, Eleni, called out, "Spiridon, keep going. For me. For Greece!" She handed him pieces of orange to soothe his parched throat.

Gathering his remaining strength, he put on a spurt.

'It was too much for Flack. Hearing footsteps behind him, he staggered and fell.'

Samuel cheered. 'You can do it! You can do it, Louis! Keep going!'

'Back at the stadium,' continued his uncle, 'the spectators had no idea who was in the lead. Finally, a cyclist arrived to announce that Flack the Australian was heading for home. The entire stadium groaned. All eyes were fixed on the tunnel leading into the arena.

'Suddenly, a man wearing a dusty white Greek vest with the number 17 entered. No one else was in sight. The stadium erupted to cheers and cries of

"A Greek! A Greek!" Spiridon Louis broke the string on the finishing line, bowed to the King of Greece and stood to attention as the band struck up the Greek national anthem.'

'Hooray! Hooray!' Samuel cried.

'It was over seven minutes before the second man, Vasilakos, ran into the arena, closely followed by the Hungarian. Six Greeks – no foreigners – followed them at intervals. The last man finished a good hour after the winner. Louis had run the first Olympic marathon in under three hours – 2 hours, 58 minutes and 50 seconds.

'As Louis was led away, asking only for a cup of black coffee to refresh himself, Queen Olga of Greece shook his rough hand and removed the gold rings from her fingers. "Here, take them," she said. "The honour you bring Greece is worth far more than these rings!" Louis had won Greece's only medal of the Games.'

Uncle Sabata sat back with a smile, seeing his nephew's eyes glisten with delight.

'Lucky man,' he murmured.

'Not so, my son,' sighed the Chief. 'Fame and fortune do not always bring happiness. Spiridon married Eleni and had two sons. He never ran a race again. Later he fell on hard times and spent a year in prison. Soon after, Eleni died and he took up work again as a water-carrier. But he was not entirely forgotten. Years later, he was invited to the 1936 Games to carry his nation's flag into the stadium. He died four years later. His name will never be forgotten. Spiridon Louis, after all, was the first man to win the Olympic marathon.'

Samuel felt exhausted after the story. It was as if he'd run the race himself, living every moment of it, experiencing the thrills and the pain of those runners long ago. There and then he vowed that one day he would run an Olympic marathon.

But how? Only white men were allowed to run for South Africa. . .

CHAPTER ELEVEN

Over longer distances, Samuel always ran alone. He reckoned that all long-distance runners must be loners. They ran, accelerated, slowed down, overtook, fell back when their bodies dictated. You cannot run a marathon of twenty-six miles at someone else's pace. No breath to chat. No time to relax for two hours. To reach the top, he would have to sacrifice friendship and family.

His running track beyond the village was a desolate plain, as hot as a furnace in the late afternoon. Once past the green of the village hollow, he was running on rocks that had been baked to dust. Far in the distance, in the borderlands close to Botswana, were the jagged red peaks of mountains overlooking the Kalahari Desert. Sometimes the air was full of gritty dust that swirled about him, covering everything in a pale yellow shroud. When a storm blew up, it forced dust into his eyes, nose and ears, blinding and deafening him.

Yet he never stopped to wipe his face. Now and again, the winds brought showers of rain that turned the dust underfoot to mud which the sun baked hard in its red-hot oven. The soles of his feet were soon as tough as elephant hide, but there was always the danger that he might sprain an ankle.

When the showers turned to torrents, rain would wash over the baked mud and disappear through cracks in the earth. But rain was scarce, and with so little water, the soil was barren with tiny islands of dry grass yellowing like spilled goat's milk. Because there was so little grass to eat, Uncle Sabata's young shepherds constantly had to take the goats out to pastures new. In the rainy season, however, the eucalyptus trees would fill the air with their oily, soothing scent and Sam would swallow the fragrance in hungry gulps.

Whenever Sam went running in the cool of the evening, Uncle Sabata would be waiting for him afterwards, chiding, praising, asking questions: 'How do you feel? Did you get stitch? Cramp? Did you do warm-up exercises as I instructed? Have you cooled down?'

Always the same.

After a long run, Sam would often rest inside

Aunt Priscilla's hut, panting, getting his breath back, breathing in the coolness of the mud walls and straw roof. Aunt Priscilla would be seated at her wooden loom, guiding the shuttle with a wide sweep of her arm and pedalling smoothly in the half-light.

One Sunday, after their morning run, Uncle Sabata summoned his nephew to his royal rondavel for a talk about the future. Sam knew what was coming. Any day now, since he'd just passed his sixteenth birthday, he would be part of his uncle's quota for the mines. Goodbye, goats – hello, gold!

But to his surprise, the Chief had other thoughts on his mind.

'You've a rare talent, my boy,' he began thoughtfully, puffing on his pipe.

Samuel wondered what was to come. Talent for what? Herding goats? Killing puff-adders? Catching bush pigs? He waited patiently for his talent to be revealed.

'I'm a good judge,' continued Uncle Sabata. 'With the right sort of handling, you'd go far.'

Once more, a long silence amid clouds of purple smoke.

'Handling for what, *Tatamkhulu*?'

His uncle stared at him.

'Why, running, of course! It's in your genes. You take after me. When I was at college I won a silver cup for the cross-country and the paper-chase.'

Samuel held his tongue. He wanted to say: yes, if you'd let me go to school, I too might have gone to college and won cups!

'Did you ever run for your country?' he asked.

Uncle Sabata said nothing for a while, then he muttered half under his breath, as if someone might hear him, 'We had runners who could have beaten anyone of any colour. They never got a chance to show what they could do. The white laws stopped them running against whites.'

'Maybe Africans aren't as good as whites,' his nephew suggested.

The Chief took the pipe from his mouth and knocked out the ash on a wooden platter. Closing his eyes, he pursed his lips, took a deep breath and cleared his throat. Then he stood up and took down a heavy book from the shelf.

'Do you see these rings?' he said, showing the book's cover to the puzzled boy.

'Yes, *Tatamkhulu*. I see five rings.'

'What colours are they?'

'Red, green, black, yellow, blue.'

'Good. What else do you see?'

'Nothing. . . except they are linked, one inside the other.'

'Precisely. They represent the five continents. Not separate, but linked together. Now, tell me, what colour is the ring in the middle?'

'Black, *Tatamkhulu.*'

'Black for Africa. Got it? Right at the start of the modern Olympics, the founder, Baron Coubertin, believed the Games should unite all nations, all colours.'

He sighed.

'But it didn't work out like that. For many years, the white bosses of the Olympics kept black Africans out of their Games as if they were their own private garden. Let me read you what one of their presidents, Baillet-Latour, had to say.'

He thumbed through the fat book until he located the page he wanted.

'Ah, here we are: "Africans should first practise sports in their own countries to learn how to play them, before applying to join the Olympic movement." Here's what other whites said: "Blacks are by nature like children, emotional and unstable. They aren't mature enough yet to compete with whites. . . When black Africans can prove they are as stable and committed to sport as athletes of Olympic nations, we might reconsider our decision."'

'So no black athletes could run in the Olympic Games?' Samuel asked.

'Oh yes, they did. Not only did they take part, they won and set new records. But those blacks did not come from Africa. They were from America and the West Indies. In 1936, the black American Jesse Owens won four gold medals on the track – in front of the Nazi leader, Adolf Hitler, who believed blacks were born inferior to the white Aryan race. Jesse certainly gave him one in the eye, and Hitler stormed out of the stadium!'

'Didn't any black African nation try to join the Olympics?' his nephew asked.

'One did. Ethiopia. Yet each time it entered, its application was turned down. No black Africans took part in the London Olympics of 1948, nor at Helsinki in 1952. It was only in 1956 that, at long last, Ethiopia's application was accepted – mainly with the support of communist countries like Russia and some newly independent African nations.

'Those Melbourne Games saw the first African runner win the marathon. His name was Alain

Mimoun. But he was running for France, despite being a native of Algeria in North Africa. At last the dam had burst. . .'

Uncle Sabata pursed his lips, blowing bubbles as if to demonstrate the torrents of water flooding the Olympics. He gave a broad smile of satisfaction, refilled his pipe and sat back in his chair.

'I am going to tell you a story,' he said in a quieter voice.

The lad sat on the floor, eager to hear more.

CHAPTER TWELVE

'I'm going to tell you about the first black African to win an Olympic gold medal in the marathon. It's an incredible story, one to inspire us all, even more than that of Spiridon Louis, because this athlete was *ours* and he won the hardest race of all – the marathon. His name was Abebe Bikila and he came from Ethiopia in the north. He did more than win the marathon in 1960; he won it in 1964 too, the only man to win twice.

'Just like you, Abebe started as a goatherd. He loved running. He used to think that if he ran for long enough, he'd reach the distant mountains before the sun did. If he could do that, the day would last for ever and he'd stop the sun from sinking into its mountain lake. And just like you, Abebe lived in a mud hut with a straw roof. By day he guarded his family's goats from wolves and jackals. Apart from his mother's loom, the goats were all that the family possessed.'

Taking another book from the top shelf, Uncle Sabata found the page he wanted and started to read to the excited youngster sitting before him.

'Abebe's father, Bikila Demassie, had been a soldier, fighting against the Italians in World War II; he wanted his son to follow in his footsteps. So, when Abebe was seventeen, his father asked the village scribe to write to the royal palace with a request that he become a soldier in the Imperial Guard of the Emperor, Haile Selassie. A year later, they received a reply, instructing the young man to come to the royal barracks in the capital, Addis Ababa.

'Abebe set off on foot from his village on the plains. He walked for many days, sleeping each night under the stars. When at last he reached the highway, he got a lift from a man with a donkey cart piled high with straw.

'Abebe became a private in the Imperial Guard, and met its PE instructor, Onni Niskanen. The Swede had been hired by the emperor who believed that Ethiopian runners could become the best in the world. Abebe learned valuable lessons from Niskanen; and he never forgot his advice:

"Run tall, extending your legs through the full range of motion.

"Relax when you're running. A runner who is too stiff shortens his stride.

"Don't waste energy by running upwards instead of forwards.

"Too much tension in the arms and shoulders stops you running fast."

'One other piece of advice remained in Abebe's memory: "Take it easy. Let others sort themselves out. Stay in touch, but don't push. Wait till the leaders tire and think that you've nothing left. That's the moment to strike."

'Niskanen soon spotted Abebe's natural ability. Yet when he held trials to choose two runners for the 1960 Olympic marathon in Rome, twenty-eight-year-old Abebe only came third. So he wasn't included in the team. At the very last moment, however, with the plane waiting on the tarmac, a jeep rushed up with bad news: one of the marathon runners had broken his ankle playing football. Niskanen had to make a split-second decision. "Go and fetch Abebe," he said.

'So it was that the experienced Mamo Wolde and the unknown Abebe Bikila were Ethiopia's entrants for the marathon. When they arrived in Rome, another problem arose: there were no running shoes to fit Abebe. So, with only a couple of hours left before the race started, he decided to run barefoot, as he did at home. No one had run an Olympic marathon without shoes before. It was a huge risk. He would be running over the sharp, slippery cobblestones of Roman streets and squares, not hard-baked mud.

'To avoid the early afternoon heat, the start was to be late in the day, which meant it would be dark in the latter stages of the race – not a good time for barefoot running. The problem was solved, however, by hundreds of bearers holding torches to light up the night sky.

'Towards the end of the race, two athletes were in the lead: the red-hot favourite from Morocco, Rhadi, and the unknown African, Abebe Bikila. Less than a mile from the finish, Abebe put on a spurt, opening up a small gap. It took the world champion Rhadi by surprise; he began to falter as the gap grew, and Abebe raced down the road where his ancestors had been driven as slaves. As he approached the finish a full twenty-six seconds ahead of Rhadi, he raised his arms wide and smiled – a great big smile. Not only had he won, he had beaten the world marathon record, coming home in 2 hours, 15 minutes and 16.2 seconds. He was the first black African to win an Olympic running event.'

Uncle Sabata's look of satisfaction turned to sadness.

'Not long after returning home as a hero, Abebe found his life turned upside down by another twist of fate. He was thrown into gaol and faced the hangman's rope! A rebellion backed by the palace guard had broken out against the emperor, and the Olympic hero fell under suspicion. Although he was eventually released, he lost his job and faced poverty with his wife and young son. Running marathons was the only way to survive.

'In the three years after the Rome Olympics he ran some thirty marathons – and won them all. He came first in the Tokyo Olympic marathon in 1964 with a new world record of 2:12:11, a whole four minutes before the second man, Britain's Basil Heatley. Once more he returned home a hero, the first man to win an Olympic marathon twice.

'Although he entered the Olympic marathon in Mexico in 1968, he cracked a bone in his right leg and had to drop out after thirteen miles. He had run his last marathon. Five months later, he crashed his car into a ditch and became paralysed from the waist down. He died three years later. He was only 41.'

Uncle Sabata shut the book with a bang.

'That, boy, is the great Abebe Bikila, a son of Africa and an inspiration to us all. Never forget him. Think of him when you run. He did it for Africans like you to follow.'

Samuel said nothing. His head was too full of running.

If Bikila could do it, why couldn't he?

CHAPTER THIRTEEN

The day was fast approaching when Samuel would leave village life to dig gold on the Reef. He was off to the gold mines at Mpumalanga with a letter of introduction for the chief *induna*. And when his holidays came, he returned to the Homelands for two weeks at harvest-time, to set up house with a wife chosen for him by the Chief. That was his destiny and his family duty.

Uncle Sabata introduced him to a shy young girl: 'This is Sinthee, your new wife,' he said.

'Thank you, Tatamkulu,' said Sam, before turning to look at his bride.

Fifteen-year-old Sinthee had been brought all the way from a distant tribal reserve beside the Indian Ocean. Poor girl, it was like taking a kitten away from its mother too early. Samuel did what he could to console her; he took his husbandly duties seriously – or, rather, he treated his child bride as a father would an illiterate country girl who missed her home and family.

A couple of days after moving with Sinthee into their own hut, Sam went back to the mines. Sinthee accepted his departure as meekly as she had accepted their marriage, but she could not help shedding a tear when left alone in the hut. Of course, the other women would help her. But she was lonely among all these strangers. Even her husband was something of a stranger to her.

Uncle Sabata wanted his nephew to continue running, so he asked the headman to find Sam an office job like his brother, rather than risk injury by digging underground. But even with a cleaning job, Sam's life was tougher than being a shepherd. For a start, the offices were rusty tin shacks built into the mine face, clinging to rugged rock. The mine was all dust and dirt – no trees, no bushes, no grass, no fresh air.

All day long, men stood over giant power drills that jangled and roared, making them shake even when they were lying in bed afterwards. Dust constantly clogged their nostrils as in a sandstorm; the earth often shook from dynamite blasts. Sam saw workers in dusty overalls stagger off into the dusk, back to wooden barracks where they would wash their grimy hands and faces in cold water as best they could. The barracks were lined with hundreds of concrete bunks built in two tiers, just a few inches from one other. Their mattresses were straw mats, their wardrobes nails in the rafters.

All day long, the overseers yelled, '*Kom, jong! Kom, jong! Ons moet werk! Tyd is geld! Tyd is geld!* Come on, boy! Come on, boy! You must work! You must work! Time is money! Time is money!'

That was gold-mining: back-breaking, ear-shattering, soul-destroying work, with nothing but a concrete slab on which to rest after a twelve-hour shift, six and a half days a week. And all to line the pockets of the white mine owners and the tribal chiefs who had sold them to the mine.

Sunday afternoon was the workers' only free time. Most men took no more recreation than hauling their weary bodies onto their bunks, but some played football or boxed in the gym. Despite his tiredness, Samuel joined the running club and tried all distances – from 100-yard sprints to 10-mile cross-countries. He always ran in bare feet. Running shoes had not been top of the shopping list when Uncle Sabata went to town for provisions and tobacco for his pipe.

Sam had made friends at the club with a Zulu lad of his own age. Simeon was a tall, lanky youth who worked on the gold-streaked rock face, nearly a mile underground. Their languages, Xhosa and Zulu, were close enough for the two to converse, and they shared a love of running. Others soon dubbed the odd pair 'Lofty' and 'Titch'. It was 'Lofty' who nagged his pal to run in plimsolls.

'Look, man, training in your bare feet is fine, if that's what suits you. But in a race, you're likely to slip arse over belly on greasy ground. What you need is something solid under you. Save up your rand, man, and get yourself some decent *takkies*.'

But Samuel loved to feel the earth beneath his feet.

'I'm used to my toes digging into warm soil,' he told Simeon. 'It makes me feel I'm at one with Mother Earth. Shoes aren't natural.'

'Look, man,' his friend persisted, 'd'you know why whites treat us like animals? Because we run like wild dogs in our bare feet. If we want to beat whites at their own game, we need to compete on equal terms.'

Samuel took some convincing. 'But. . . Abebe Bikila won an Olympic marathon bare-footed.'

In the end, Simeon won him over by simple reasoning. 'If ever we're allowed to compete against whites, they won't let you run in bare feet. You know what the white *baas* is like: all blazer and badges. Clean shirt, shorts, socks and shoes, like an English gentleman. They'd run in top hat and tails if they could. *But not bare feet!*'

A week later, Samuel tried on his first pair of running shoes. The shoe agent said he'd never seen feet like Sam's before: 'Your soles and heels are as hard as rocks, boy!'

It took him months to get used to plimsolls. At first he hated his footwear: he felt like a cheetah running in army boots. In his first race he tripped over his own feet, fell with a crash and came last, bloodied and bruised. That wasn't the only mishap. Once he stubbed his toe on a stone and brought down another runner on top of him. How that man cursed the country boy!

'Bloody *kaffir*!' he shouted, as he picked himself up and limped on. 'You shouldn't be allowed to run with civilised athletes!'

'Ignore him,' said Simeon, stopping to help Sam up. 'The best way to deal with such people is to beat them.' He laughed. 'Not over the head with a *takkie*, but in the race.'

The two friends ran together, helping each other – first one leading, then the other. With just a hundred yards to go, they caught up their rival and finished in the leading group.

'Who's the *kaffir* now?' muttered Simeon, out of earshot of the beaten runner.

Slowly but surely, Samuel got used to running with his feet wrapped in rubber and cloth. To his surprise, he found that his running improved and he started to be noticed. He attracted the attention of an old white coach hired by the mine to train young miners for local races. It was the first time he had received advice from an experienced coach.

The grizzled old fellow shattered his dreams. 'You're all wrong for long distances, man,' he said bluntly. 'Switch to boxing or wrestling amongst the featherweights.'

He saw the youngster's look of disappointment.

'Look, boy,' he tried to explain. 'You're too small. Long distance runners are tall and stringy, like your mate Simeon. Your shape's all cock-eyed. You lean too far forward, you run on the balls of your feet rather than toe-heel, toe-heel. You don't pace yourself – you use up too much energy in short bursts. You've no finishing speed. Don't waste your time, man. Forget running.'

Who was Samuel to believe? Bikila's coach had said, 'Lean forward,' and, 'Run on the balls of your feet.' Now old Jan Smit was saying the opposite. What the coach didn't spot was Sam's stubbornness. He was determined to prove the coach wrong. If Mr Smit wouldn't take him on, fine, he'd train himself, running as it suited him. Sometimes he'd run with Simeon, but his friend did shift work and rarely finished before six or seven in the evening. So Sam began to run long distances alone, beyond the mine, farther and farther, so that eventually he'd notch up as much as two hundred miles a week. He would pace the distance between trees or telegraph poles: two fast, one steady, two fast, one steady. He healed his sprains with herbs and massaged his legs with his own sinewy fingers.

When Samuel felt ready, he suggested to Simeon that they enter their first competitive races against black runners from other mines: first five miles, then ten, fifteen, twenty. . .

Simeon agreed. 'We can work as a two-man team,' he said. 'We'll take turns setting the pace and break up the rhythm of the other runners.'

The running tracks weren't like those Sam had heard about at clubs or private schools reserved for whites. These tracks were mud and weeds in the shadow of mine landfills. If you were lucky, someone had painted white lines to indicate 'Start' and 'Finish', or put traffic cones on the inside to keep you on the right track.

In their very first race, both went sprawling in the mud. Just before the start there'd been a torrential downpour, and their plimsolls squelched and slithered all over the place. But they helped each other up, brushed themselves down and set off in pursuit of the field.

Although neither won many races – in fact, Samuel came last more than once, especially over shorter distances where speed was a factor – they were improving all the time. The most valuable lesson was patience. Samuel was the wise tortoise racing against the impetuous hare. He would bide his time, preserve his strength for the second part of the race and wear his opponents down. Simeon was more the gazelle, bounding easily and gracefully over the ground, keeping an even pace for mile upon mile. What he lacked was 'killer instinct', the ability to accelerate and hunt down his prey over long distances.

'If I had your stamina,' he'd tell his companion, 'I'd be a champion.'

'And if I had your speed, I'd beat the world,' Samuel would add.

'Among blacks,' Simeon would remind him.

Sam shook his head.

'The day is coming, Simeon, when we'll take on whites and beat them. Mark my words. You and me. "Lofty and Titch", we'll call ourselves!'

Within a year, the two 17-year-olds were gaining a reputation as decent long-distance runners. While 'Lofty' became champion of Crown Mine No. 3 at anything from five to ten miles, 'Titch' invariably outlasted him on 15-mile cross-countries. Mine officials began to enter them against other mines. Not only did running earn them better rations, it gave them time off for training and competing. No one benefited more than Simeon. In winter, he saw daylight for the first time, even spent an entire week above ground. He started to put meat on his bony frame.

At the end of their second year at the mine, they entered their first marathon. It was at the annual miners' gala. Samuel had run the five-mile race the previous day and come fourth, higher than ever before. Simeon, however, won the race in a sprint for the line, his lanky legs taking him clear of the second man.

The marathon was scheduled for the gala's final day and it seemed that all the runners, including the two friends, were going to run the course. Fifty lined up at the start, some of them hopefuls in good spirits, as if this was a country ramble. But a few were seasoned long-distance men who'd already covered the marathon distance.

'At least we don't have to run heats to qualify,' said Simeon. 'My legs wouldn't stand it. I might win one dash for the finishing line, but not two.'

'Don't worry,' said Samuel. 'I can't imagine a mad scramble for the line after twenty-six miles, can you? The winning time is likely to be minutes over other runners, not split seconds. Remember, this is an endurance test. Pace yourself, relax, let yourself be carried along by the crowd.'

Simeon grimaced. This was twice as far as he'd ever run before.

Samuel wondered how he would do. Would his legs or lungs fail him? Did he have the mental strength? He would soon find out whether the marathon was his race or not.

The two friends kept together for over half the race. But by that time three things were clear. First, in a marathon everyone has to run at their own pace, slowing for a breather when they need to, speeding up when they feel refreshed, taking a drink when their throat runs dry. He could not run at Simeon's pace, any more than Simeon could run at his. The second realisation was that he found it easy to sustain a regular rhythm; it was taking him past other runners until only three were ahead. Another couple of miles, and two of the leaders were slowing down, unable to keep up the pace.

The third discovery was the most satisfying of all. Samuel was loving the marathon. This was the distance he was born to run. He had enjoyed running alone across the veld, but it lacked the competitive spirit. Here he could hunt down his rivals, stalk them as they floundered and overtake them with ease.

With just a mile to go, there was no sign of Simeon. Samuel couldn't slow down to wait for him to catch up – for all he knew, his friend might have dropped out. After twenty-six miles he still felt strong and had enough energy in reserve to put in a spurt. That took him past the leader and soon opened up a 100-yard gap which he maintained until the finishing line. His first marathon. His first victory!

'Lofty' and 'Titch' were not only the best of running pals, they spoke frankly to each other in their native tongue – when out of earshot of police agents. Samuel was able to try out on Simeon the ideas taking shape in his mind. Both hated the racist policies of the white government. But what were they to do? How do you put an end to Apartheid? Sam recalled the two people with opposing views on the train, years earlier. The man had been right to say that blacks had to organise themselves and fight back. But the woman had been right too. Those in power had the strongest army in Africa, and they'd use force when they needed to, as he knew only too well.

Simeon told Samuel about things he knew nothing of.

'Have you heard of the liberation struggle?' he asked one day, as they were jogging together.

'I've heard talk of people who want to set us free from white rule.'

'Yes, we comrades have a political party to lead us, the ANC. Some of its leaders are in prison.'

Samuel was puzzled.

'They can't fight in prison.'

'Yes, but others can take their place.'

'Words alone won't help us.'

'True enough. But we have weapons. And our comrades are being trained in friendly countries.'

'Where?' asked Samuel, full of curiosity.

'Oh, here and there. It's top secret. The ANC has a secret military organisation fighting the white regime. It blows up power stations, raids munition dumps to get weapons – that sort of thing. They call it *Umkhonto we Sizwe* – Spear of the Nation. It includes any comrade opposed to Apartheid, white as well as black. The leader is a white man, a communist, called Joe Slovo.'

Samuel was impressed, but he didn't see the point of using spears against guns.

Simeon smiled. 'Don't let *Umkhonto* fool you. Behind every spear is a gun, a bomb, even a tank or plane if needed.'

Sam shook his head.

'I'll let my feet do the shooting. One day, when whites are forced to race against us, we'll prove who's stronger and faster.'

Simeon stuck to his guns. Literally. One day he vanished into the blue, leaving a brief note for his friend:

Gone to pick up my spear.
Good luck, comrade.
Win for us.
Simeon.

• • •

In the next couple of years, Samuel sowed the first seeds of a family, leaving Sinthee to bring up their two daughters. Each time he returned to the mine, his growing family pulled at his heart-strings.

'I hate to leave you, Sinthee,' he explained. 'I know how hard it is for you to bring up the girls on your own. But I must earn money to repay Uncle Sabata and feed you and our girls.'

Sinthee was silent. Tears made silver tracks down her cheeks and fell onto the backs of her brown hands.

'Please don't cry,' he said, putting his arm round her shoulders. 'One day you'll be proud of me, I promise you. I'm going to run for our country. That's my dream. . . No, that's my *intention*. It will be my contribution to the struggle.'

'The whites won't allow it,' she said in a shaking voice.

'Then I must show them they are wrong. Besides, running will bring us enough money to live together. I'll buy you a transistor radio. You'll see.'

Sinthee smiled through her tears.

'I'm with you, husband, whatever you do.'

On his twice-yearly trips home to see his family, Samuel had to give a full report of his running to Uncle Sabata. It was as if the Chief were living the dream he'd once had himself.

'I told you, boy,' he'd say. 'I said you'd make a good runner.'

And Samuel would reply, 'I don't want to be a runner. I want to be a champion.'

CHAPTER FOURTEEN

Because the two brothers worked at different mines, Sam never got to see Looksmart except during their two-week harvest break in the Homelands. One day, however, the *induna* handed Samuel a long buff envelope with unfamiliar words stamped across the top in black ink:

SOUTH AFRICAN PRISON SERVICE
GRADE 1 SECURITY

Down the side, in even larger black letters, was a stamp:

CENSORED

Sam's hands trembled as he opened the envelope and pulled out a single thin sheet of paper. It contained just three short paragraphs of tightly-written text, as if the writer wanted to squeeze as much on to one page as possible. There had obviously been several more sentences, but someone had blacked out half the page.

Samuel's eyes at once went to the address in the top right-hand corner. . . He could hardly believe what he saw:

> Looksmart Gqibela – D491/64,
> c/o The Officer Commanding,
> Robben Island Prison,
> ROBBEN ISLAND 8000.

Between the black censored passages were the following words:

My dear Samuel ,

As you see, I am no longer a clerk in the mines. I now dig rocks in a quarry. A merry old job that keeps me busy and helps the time go by.

I was tried and charged with sabotage and conspiracy to overthrow the government by revolution. I do not xxxxxx [for six lines]

I was also charged with assisting an armed invasion of South Africa. What xxxxx [for five lines]

The judge sentenced me to 18 years imprisonment. That was over a year ago. But xxxxx *[for ten lines]*

I arrived here in the middle of winter. It's a rocky island washed by angry seas, damp and bitterly cold now. Thick mists roll in off the South Atlantic. Yet on a clear day I can see Table Mountain and ships sailing to and from Cape Town, seven miles away.

The island has its own wild beauty: deer and ostrich, seal and penguin, yellow bushes and sweet-smelling eucalyptus trees.

My cell is xxxxx *[for three lines]*

In the evening I read and talk with other prisoners. There are some big names here. . . xxxxx *[for three lines]*

I am permitted a visit once every six months. I've had only one visitor – Nicky. But he won't be back for some time.

Write and tell me your news.

Your loving brother,

Looksmart

P.S. When you write, your letter must be no more than 500 words

You could have knocked Samuel down with a fly whisk! Looksmart, with a secure clerk's position at the mine. Looksmart, who had been chosen by Uncle Sabata to be the future Tribal Chief. Looksmart – now in gaol for eighteen years! He'd be getting on for forty when he was let out! An old man.

And Looksmart wasn't just in prison. He was on Robben Island. Sam knew from people at the mine that Robben Island was a secure place for highly dangerous prisoners such as Nelson Mandela and Walter Sisulu, leaders of the African National Congress. Was Looksmart really that important?

So his brother had joined the Struggle. Looky had vowed to take revenge for the family's killing. And he'd evidently kept his promise. He was now a political prisoner alongside Mandela!

The shock of having a dangerous criminal for a brother was one thing. But it wasn't long before Sam received another brotherly blow. Early one Sunday morning, as he was getting up for his morning run, he was startled by a knocking at the door of his broom cupboard of a room. Not a knock-knock, but a sharp *Dit. Di-di-di-di. Dit-dit!* The noise took him back to his township days, where boys had used that knock as a code: 'Safe to open up'.

'Who's there?' he called nervously.

'John Wayne,' came a deep voice.

Nicky!

Sam pulled open the door.

The visitor didn't have a horse or a Winchester rifle. But he did have the lop-sided grin and cowboy swagger Sam knew so well.

'Howdy, pardner!' he said, glancing down the corridor as if a Mohawk hunting party was on his trail.

He hopped into the room, closing the door behind him.

'Well, well,' he muttered, grabbing his brother in a bear hug. 'Lookee here! The mine air suits you, little brother. See how big you've grown.'

Sam couldn't say that the air suited Nicky. As he flopped back on the bed, his crutch clattered onto the concrete floor.

'Got any grub?' he asked, shutting his eyes.

Samuel spread his rations out on the blanket. Nicky's hungry eyes devoured the lot, but his mouth chewed slowly on the stringy goat *biltong* and dried fruit. While he concentrated on the food, Sam took a good look at him. He was shocked by what he saw.

Nicky's greasy overalls were full of holes; one ragged trouser leg was pinned up above the knee. His chin and cheeks were covered in thick woolly undergrowth and he resembled a desperado being hunted down by the Sheriff's men. His forehead was deeply furrowed. His hands were blotchy and scarred. Yet when he opened his eyes, it was the same old Nicky: cheeky, crafty, bubbling over with hopes and impossible dreams.

All the same, there was a new steely glint in the once-soft brown eyes.

'Don't they feed you at home?' Samuel said, to break the silence.

Nicky stared long and hard at him, as a seasoned sergeant would at a raw recruit still wet behind the ears. When he spoke, his words were unexpected.

'Whose side are you on, little brother?'

Sam didn't know what to say.

'Our. . . side. Your. . . side,' he stuttered, unsure what was meant.

'You're still young. . .' Nicky murmured.

'I'll soon be nineteen!' Samuel cried. 'I can read and write, even if I didn't finish school. I can milk goats. I have a wife and two children. I have won cups for running. I'm training to be a champion.'

Nicky laughed into his beard.

'Good for you. Champion, eh? That'll put the wind up old whitey.'

Realisation slowly dawned on Samuel.

'Are you a terrorist?'

Nicky put a grubby finger to his lips.

'Comrade, yes. Soldier, yes. Terrorist, no. Don't breathe a word. When I got out of hospital I knew what I had to do. All I thought of was getting my revenge. Fighting back. So I joined a liberation army unit. At first, they didn't want a one-legged bandit like me. But I soon showed them I could run as fast as them. And I could be useful: the police didn't suspect a cripple. . . not until it was too late and I'd blown up a few strategic targets.'

'What are "strategic targets"?'

'You're better not knowing,' his brother said with a frown. He changed the subject: 'Have you heard from Looksmart?'

Samuel told Nicky about the letter.

'He's been moved to the mainland,' said Nicky. 'Dunno where, exactly; my sources didn't say.'

'Can we see him?'

'No. Not until he gets better . . . *if* he gets better. His mind became badly damaged on Robben Island. He wouldn't recognise us.'

The two brothers sat in silence for several minutes.

It was Nicky who broke the silence.

'We'll make them pay! Keep the faith, comrade.'

Pulling himself up, he brushed the crumbs from

his overalls and gave his brother a hug. 'Must go, little brother. Mustn't stay too long in one place. See you soon. After liberation. Very soon. . .'

He opened the door a few inches and, seeing the coast was clear, hopped out and swung down the corridor on his crutch. Before turning the corner, he looked back with his lop-sided grin, his clenched fist punching the air.

So Nicky had joined the Struggle. A one-legged soldier, on the run, taking out 'strategic targets'. What would happen when the police caught him? No one escaped their clutches for long.

Mum would have been proud. What on earth would Dad have said? Two sons, two rebels! And what would Mum and Dad have said about their youngest son being a running champion? Mum's face would wrinkle with delight, but Dad would surely disapprove. Blacks had to know their place, where Dad was concerned. He used to say that whites were cut out to play cricket and bowls because they dressed in white. Samuel had never agreed with Dad's old-fashioned ideas.

● ● ●

A couple of months later, his eye caught a headline in the office newspaper:

ONE-LEGGED TERRORIST KILLED
IN SHOOT-OUT WITH POLICE

Below was a picture of a body in torn, one-legged dungarees lying in the gutter. Samuel recognised it at once, though the paper didn't give the man's name. It just called him 'the Black Assassin'.

So Nicky had never lived to see the freedom he was fighting for.

Sam broke down in tears.

There and then, he decided to become a comrade, to be part of the Struggle. Yet Nicky's death reinforced his decision to fight for freedom in his own way. By using his natural gift. Every victory would be a blow for freedom, a victory for all South Africans, white as well as black.

CHAPTER FIFTEEN

After three years as a miner, something happened that was to change Samuel's life – and that of every other South African. Following a long struggle, the white government gave in. On 2nd February 1990, it freed all political prisoners, including the black leader Nelson Mandela. With everyone else in the mine office, Sam crowded round the small television set as a tall, slim, grey-haired man in a smart grey suit walked through the prison gates. He was hand-in-hand with his wife Winnie.

'So that is Nelson Mandela,' thought Samuel. 'Born in the Bantu homelands, son of a tribal chief, moved to the township – the opposite journey from me. He has sacrificed family and career for the liberation struggle, and spent twenty-seven years in prison.'

Another thought struck him. 'I wonder if he ever met Looky?'

He felt a keen attachment to this dignified, elderly

man, and not only because he'd shared Robben Island with his brother. Mandela's quiet dignity persuaded Sam to serve the cause in his own way.

All along the road to Cape Town thousands of black and white people sang and danced together as Mandela's car slowly drove past. At the old City Hall, Mandela emerged onto the balcony, raised his fist in a victory salute and called out to the thousands below, '*Mayibuye iAfrika!* May Africa return!'

In the year following the release of political prisoners, the Apartheid regime fell apart rapidly. Once the government had abolished the last racist laws, South Africa was readmitted to the Olympic movement on 9 July 1991. Now South African athletes – blacks, Indians, Coloureds and whites – were free to take part in the Olympic Games. A non-racial team could compete in Barcelona in the summer of 1992.

So the way was now clear for the young black runner to realise his dream of representing his country. On a visit to the tribal reserve, he told Uncle Sabata of his plans.

'Hold your horses, boy,' said the Chief. 'So you think non-whites will compete equally with whites, do you? And in a year's time? Have you ever seen a black woman playing hockey or netball, doing gymnastics, swimming or diving? Have you seen black men sailing yachts, shooting pistols or cycling? No, of course you haven't. Even if they start now they won't reach Olympic qualifying standards in under a year. It'll take donkey's years.'

Samuel's face fell. He was still too young and raw to run an Olympic marathon, but he hoped to do it one day. He didn't know how long 'donkey's years' was, but he was determined to be ready for the Olympics when his chance came.

At the mine, he managed to catch the opening ceremony of the Olympic Games on television. The South African commentator let them know what the rest of the world did not: that when the new South African team marched into the Olympic Stadium, the mix of blacks and whites in the squad was for appearance's sake only. Twenty-five black athletes, with black marathon runner Jan Tau at their head, had been permitted to march, even though they could not compete – because they had not reached the qualifying standards. This was a gesture of what the new nation wanted to be, not what it was.

No one from South Africa won a gold medal.

Samuel followed the marathon on television. He

felt as if his feet were pounding the streets, his elbows were guarding his space as his arms pumped hard, his lungs breathing in the dusty air. As if he were toiling up the final hill: shorter strides now, quick breaths like a swimmer, making fast bursts to break the Korean and the Japanese in front of him. It was his green and gold vest that breasted the tape. . . in his dreams.

But he was only twenty-one. No one had ever won an Olympic marathon at such a tender age. Bikila had won his first gold at twenty-eight, his last at thirty-two. Sam would have to bide his time, train hard, gather experience.

● ● ●

Two years later, the mine workers were given the day off to do something extraordinary. For the first time in their lives, black people were going to vote. Samuel was more excited than he'd ever been in his life. He wouldn't miss voting for the world, even though he was registered in a township outside Johannesburg. On election day he had to take a bus to his election ward and join the long queue. It wound back four miles, inching forward along dusty, pot-holed tracks linking shanty town to shanty town. Everywhere he saw slogans saying:

AMANDLA
LONG LIVE THE ANC
FREEDOM

The line kept moving – slowly, at half a mile an hour – down dirt tracks lined with starving stray dogs padding along, heads down, warily eyeing this exotic human snake.

How far they'd come. A thousand years. A million miles. How far they still had to go!

Now they were approaching eGoli, 'the golden city', the richest city in all Africa. No river, no lake, no sea for four hundred miles – just gold, a mile deep inside the earth, and all that gold could buy. A million people: half white, half black, separated by fear.

Samuel stared curiously at the large, magnolia-coloured houses. Grand. Detached. In their own grounds. Surrounded by high white walls – high enough to stop anyone climbing in, low enough to let you admire the close-cropped lawns, theblue hydrangeas, flaming red roses and border splashes of marigolds. Some had a white flagpole rooted in a bed of red-tongued proteas. There were no flags flying today.

These were private homes with their own toilets and toilet rolls, light bulbs and lampshades, carpets and curtains, gas stoves and Teflon pans, upstairs bedrooms and tiled bathrooms. Not a slogan in sight, yet the very houses shouted out: '*Ons is nog steeds baas al dink jy nie so nie!* We are still the boss, whether you think so or not!'

The tarmac shimmered in the autumn sun, like sunbeams dancing in a water jug. Was this a mirage? Were they really going to slake their thirst at the well of freedom? Or would they arrive only to see the old familiar sign: WHITES ONLY?

Closer, ever closer. Almost there now. The first day of a new life, a new nation, the Rainbow Nation. Green for the trees and grassy plain through which lion and elephant, giraffe and rhino roamed. Blue for the lakes and rivers where hippo and crocodile swam. Yellow for the gold beneath the veld. Black and white for the people who lived in this colourful land. Red for blood. The same blood that flowed through the veins of all humankind. That same precious blood spilled by millions to bring about this day: 27 April, 1994.

'You must be tired. . . comrade.'

A voice behind him. A woman's voice. No clips or clicks of Xhosa, Zulu, Venda or Tsonga. He turned his head, just a swift glance before facing the front again. She was smiling shyly, uncertainly. She looked weary, though her cornflower blue eyes shone boldly, as if lit by candles.

'Aren't you tired?' No 'comrade' this time. Perhaps she felt it was insulting. So it was. What right had she to call him 'comrade'?

But, wait. Today was the day they were all starting afresh as human beings, as South Africans, as equals. As Nelson Mandela had said, they must not replace white by black prejudice. And if a man who'd spent nearly half his life in prison could forgive his tormentors, who was Sam to disagree?

They were walking along in silence, the white woman to his right, half a step behind. Her question had drifted up like fire-smoke and fizzled out in the clear blue sky. He stole a glance at her. The woman's lined features suggested she was in her late thirties – pale pink skins age quickly under an African sun. Her faded straw hair was laced with silver strands tied in a bun with red, white and blue ribbons, like bunting on an English country maypole. The loose folds of her thin, corn-coloured frock dropped down to painted pink toenails poking out from nut-brown sandals. A white matron in her true colours.

And yet. . . on her breast she'd pinned three more ribbons: green, yellow and black. *His* colours. *His* party. Samuel felt awkward. She'd called him 'comrade'; she was wearing his colours as well as her own. She'd asked if he was tired. She'd held out an olive branch and he'd dashed it from her hands. On this day of all days. Forgiveness Day.

'No,' he said huskily. He licked his lips and cleared his throat. He didn't want her to think him ignorant. She wouldn't know how poor his English was.

'No, lady,' he said. 'I not tired. I wait many years. No mind waiting bit longer.'

'My name is Susan,' she said quietly. 'I'm thirty-five.'

How odd Europeans are. Why would he want to know her name and age? He wasn't a policeman. But to be polite, he said, 'I'm twenty-three.'

'First-time voter at twenty-three,' she said, hunching her shoulders.

He wanted to say that the man he was going to vote for was seventy-six – that the man had spent twenty-seven years of his life in prison, just to win the right to vote in the land of his birth. That he had waited many, long, hard years for this day. That his people had been tear-gassed, savaged by police dogs, thrown into gaol, tortured, driven into exile, beaten to death, and seen their loved ones murdered. But. . . they had won.

These were Sam's thoughts as he walked down the road following the line, on, on, on, towards the voting station. Black, brown and white were trudging along, half-embarrassed in each other's company, excited, yet afraid that their prize would somehow be snatched away.

At last. . . Weary hands were passing him a slip of paper, pencil on a string, showing him to a black-curtained booth. There before him on the paper was a row of photos. His man was in the middle. Proud, slim, with just the hint of a smile of triumph on his lips.

With trembling fingers, Samuel picked up the pencil and put a bold, defiant X in the square beside his man. Quickly, he folded the paper and pushed it into the open mouth of the voting box. There! It was done!

He emerged from the stale air of the booth, breathing out until his lungs were empty. Then, with a great gasp, he swallowed the sweet air of freedom. He had entered the polling station nervous, unsure; he was leaving it a new man. He had shed the burden of the past: the white man's burden – the black man's burden.

He couldn't help himself. He opened his mouth and roared like a lion.

Like a madman, he jigged up and down doing a *toyi-toyi*. All around him people were cheering and singing and dancing. It was like a carnival. All those little people whom society had turned into voiceless, faceless, right-less good-for-nothings were rejoicing. They were *free*! They did count for something, after all. They were human beings. They were free to choose their own destiny.

CHAPTER
SIXTEEN

Now that the colour bar was gone, Samuel was able to enter races against the country's top athletes. Not only that – he found himself running in some of South Africa's best athletic stadiums instead of rough-and-ready open spaces, on tartan tracks instead of cinder lanes, in front of thousands of spectators instead of a few squawking kids and crows, with a starting pistol instead of a shout of 'Ready, Steady, Go!' To his surprise, some white runners greeted him as one of them, a runner, a friendly rival. Some shared their water flask with a kindly smile.

It took a while for Samuel to feel at ease among them. At first, he wondered what they were thinking. Had they spoken out against the old regime? Against the murder of black people? Against all-white teams in cricket, rugby, tennis and athletics, while the rest of the world was drawing on the best talent, black as well as white?

Nonetheless, old habits die hard. Not all his fellow runners greeted him with a smile and a hand-shake. There was one occasion when he was selected to compete in all three long-distance races in Johannesburg; he had to spend two nights in the stadium hotel. To his initial relief, he found himself in a single room while all the white athletes shared another. His happy mood turned sour, however, when it was whispered to him that no white would share a room with him. He felt like a leper.

Samuel responded in the only way he knew: on the track. He took first place in the 5,000 metres on day one, won the 10,000 metres on day two, and came third in the marathon on day three. The first two races had taken their toll and, though he was leading the marathon with a mile to go, his legs were too heavy to prevent two white runners from pipping him at the post.

Still, his performance brought him to the notice of South Africa's athletics chiefs. A year before the Olympics, he was chosen with two white athletes to run in the Honolulu Marathon. With so much political pressure on them, sports officials were desperate to include a black runner.

'It will give you experience of foreign conditions,'

they said. 'If you do well, you could be in the running for the Olympic squad.'

Sam was given a fortnight off work to prepare. He took the opportunity to see Sinthee and the kids. He needed to relax with his family, do some light running in the veld and consult Uncle Sabata on conditions abroad. He imagined Honolulu to be much like England.

Sinthee was his rock. She didn't say much. But by reassuring smiles and little loving gestures, she gave him inspiration he couldn't find elsewhere. Samuel would sit down on the hut floor and talk about his worries and hopes.

'How will I do in my first foreign race? Well enough to make the Olympic team? So much depends on it. All my grown-up life I've pledged my running to the Struggle. But what if I fail? It'll all be for nothing. What if I get an injury?'

He didn't expect a reply. But a firm voice surprised him.

'You *won't* fail, husband. As long as you pray to the spirits, they'll protect you from injury.'

'Not fail, Daddy,' echoed his eldest daughter.

Samuel now had three daughters, with another child on the way. Fanie's little voice, added to that of his wife's, made him realise how painful parting from them always was. But it strengthened his resolve to do his very best.

He had never been abroad. His journeying had taken him from his township in the suburbs of Johannesburg, on to the Bantu Homelands in the north and, finally, to the gold mine at Mpumalanga. Almost all his running – from the police as well as in races – had been in and around Jo'burg. Now, here he was at Malan Airport, dressed in a smart black blazer and white trousers, boarding a plane for the other side of the world. When he checked the map in the seat pocket before him, he was surprised to find that Honolulu was not in America at all, but in the middle of the Pacific Ocean, halfway between Japan and the USA.

And after the marathon, he wrote a letter to Sinthee. True, she couldn't read, but she'd find someone to read it to her.

Dear Wife,

Would you believe it? I won! I won! I beat the best South African whites. Not only that. I beat some of the great world longer.

And I did it my way. For the first half of the race I ran with the leading pack, never forcing the pace. After halfway, I started to put in short bursts to break up the rhythm of other runners.

The weather wasn't fit for a lizard. That helped me. A lot of Europeans and Americans dropped out through heat exhaustion. But I kept running as if I was at home chasing jackals under the midday sun.

I finished in my best time ever: two hours, sixteen minutes. That raised a few fair eyebrows, I can tell you. I could see by the surprise on their faces! Who was this little black boy who was breaking all the rules of running?

Anyway, I did it and I'm so happy.

Your Husband

When athletics chiefs came to pick three runners to go to the Olympics, Samuel was their natural choice for third spot. Not only was he likely to spare their blushes and finish the race, *he was black*. And in the new South Africa, it was good politics to include a black person in the Olympic team, whether he was a likely winner or not.

But the new sports leaders did not want merely to turn up, with a few black faces. They wished to put their country on the map and show what the world had missed during all those years of white rule. To make a decent showing, however, would cost a lot of money and their budget was tight.

More than anyone, the young miner understood the choice: food and housing for thousands of poor blacks *or* an Olympic medal. He could only justify the sports leaders' choice by considering what victory by a black South African would do for the country's morale.

Well, he'd do his very best to be that South African.

CHAPTER SEVENTEEN

Memories of running for dear life are always hard to untangle from Samuel's thoughts when he waits for a race to start. Through his head pound the boots of policemen, the whizz and whine of bullets, the screams of children as they fall, clutching head or chest. No matter how he feels about his rivals, he can never separate them from the police on his heels. He must outrun them to survive.

Samuel breathes in through his nostrils, heaving fresh air up and into his lungs. Next, he takes a deep breath into his mouth and throat; it rushes down like a stream of warm water. Smells are so different from his township. The air is foreign: iron and concrete, street muffins and cinnamon bagels, perfumed women and scented aromas from the busy stores. It is a world apart from the familiar smells of the veld: musty trails of lion and wild dog, sage and laurel that drift on the warm breeze, fresh chicken and mealies cooking in the communal pot.

The smells of the township waft into his memory: the sour stench of sewers, the long-drop lavatory at the end of the row, rotting dog carcasses, glistening slops drying on the dirt patch outside the *shebeens*, the smell of death on that unforgettable day years ago – a smell that clogs the nostrils, clings to clothing and skin, a smell that will stay with him for ever.

Here, bad smells are washed away with disinfectant. On the track his keen nose takes in the sweet smell of lubrication oil, the whiff of sweat-beads on nerve-racked bodies, the pungent breath of freshly watered, newly cropped grass.

As he glances about him, Samuel sees several runners licking their dry lips as they await the gun. It is more than the usual nerves that pump adrenalin through their veins. It is fear. A few days earlier a small pipe bomb exploded in the city, killing one person and injuring over a hundred. Sam didn't hear the bomb go off. But bombs and pistol shots are part of everyday life in the township.

The marathon runners are sitting ducks for any sniper concealed behind a concrete column. No wonder there is fear in their eyes; they can't wait to get onto the roads. But the stadium looks safe enough at this early hour.

Samuel is ready. No oils. No massage. No pep talk on tactics. But he has something no other runner possesses or even knows about: his rituals to appease the ancestral spirits. He never starts a race without praying to the spirits. At home he and his wife and children would bury a goat's heart and liver outside the hut before they went to bed. In the Olympic Village it is hard to come by a goat's heart or liver – and in any case, the corridor outside his room has a concrete floor.

But he has another charm to ward off evil spirits: his dreadlocks! They shake and sway like snakes as he runs, protecting him from the *thickoloshes* and the *baloye*. Oh yes, the dreadlocks and his ancestral spirits will help him outdo evil spirits and. . .§ who knows? Their *muti*, their magic power, might help him win.

What is going through his mind in those last seconds on the track? Like bolts of lightning, snapshots of his family and friends flash by. Thoughts of the entire village huddled round the Chief's radio, listening for a mention of their man. Just the words 'Gqibela takes the lead. . .' will raise a cheer. If only he can make it happen. . .

Thoughts of his wife Sinthee and his daughters in their mud hut outside the village, listening to the transistor radio he bought them with cash from his winnings. Will the girls hear their father's name?

Thoughts of his friends at the gold mine, snatching a moment to listen to the tannoy relaying news of the race's progress throughout Crown Mines.

Thoughts of his brother Looksmart and his old running partner Simeon. If only they could be here now! If Looky is still alive, perhaps he is listening to a radio.

In Sam's left running shoe is a single sheet of paper, folded in four. On it is a handwritten note which he knows by heart:

Good luck, comrade.
Show the world what we could have done, given half a chance. What we can do now we are free. And what great things we shall achieve in the future. Win for us, the new South Africa.
Mandiba.

His eyes mist over just to think that Nelson Mandela is with him, willing him on. Under his breath, he murmurs, 'I'll do my best, Mandiba.'

He is not the only South African competing for Olympic glory. Already Penny Heyns has won both the 100 metres and the 200 metres breast stroke in the swimming pool; and Marianne Kriel has taken bronze in the 100 metres back stroke. And Sam has watched with a fast-beating heart the first black South African to win an Olympic medal, Hezekiel Sepeng, taking silver in the 800 metres.

Two white women and one black man. It is up to Sam to even it up. Two gold, one silver, one bronze. Can he make it three gold? Two silver? Two bronze? Two black medals, three white?

The three marathon runners in green and gold have agreed to run together, to help each other through the tough times. Now, they stand within touching distance, smiling nervously to give each other courage. They will need it over the next twenty-six miles – even more so over the last three hundred and eighty-five yards.

● ● ●

PA-A-A-A-K!

A sharp retort from the starter's pistol echoes round the stadium like a crack of thunder. Samuel almost jumps out of his skin, for a split second imagining himself back home in the township. When his nerves settle, a shiver of relief spreads through his body. At last the waiting is over and he can run the tension out of his taut muscles.

A loosening lap of the track and the runners are on their way, into the wide, muggy streets. No one wants to take the lead or push the pace. Olympic rules ban 'rabbits', hired pacemakers who provide a fast ride for the 'foxes'. The entire field jogs comfortably along, eyeing each other warily in case someone makes a break. In the city's heat they are saving themselves for the second half of the race.

So it continues for the first dozen miles, with the leading pack of some fifty athletes, well over a third of the runners, bunched together like a herd of buffalo cantering across the plains. Sam tucks in, content for the moment to be carried along with the tide, conserving his strength.

At thirteen miles, halfway, an Ethiopian is in the lead. Although he is the current world record-holder for the marathon, he has been relatively quiet since his exploits eight years earlier. A shooting star who has fizzled out? Few think him a serious threat. All the same, many recall the amazing feats of Abebe Bikila and Mamo Wolde. So is this man Ethiopia's secret weapon? His halfway split time is shown on an illuminated board: 1:07:36. A snail's pace.

Someone . . . soon . . . is going to have to run some quick miles. Otherwise, the endurance men will hand the race to the 'sprinters' among them, who'll win a dash for the finishing line.

True enough, the pace begins to pick up as the runners head for home. They've done the donkey work, the first thirteen miles; they've accustomed their lungs and legs to the heat and asphalt. Now it's time to focus on running fast enough to stay in the leading pack, yet preserving enough energy for the last gut-wrenching three miles.

The leading group starts to thin out until there are thirteen athletes running almost abreast. The South African trio hold: the two, tall muscular white men and the skinny little black fellow.

Most eyes are fixed on the favourites, the big names, who are in the leading group. The cream is beginning to rise to the top.

All the same, as the runners pass the 15-mile marker, it is still anybody's race. Eleven miles to go.

Then something unprecedented happens. As planned, the three green-and-gold men strike out for home, taking turns to force the pace, dragging each other along and trying to break up the rhythm of their rivals. Those watching on television back home dare wonder if the impossible can happen: an unheard-of gold, silver and bronze. What a feat that would be!

Spectators litter the avenues outside McDonald's, Kentucky Fried Chicken and Starbucks, munching burgers and doughnuts. Brown and pink, women and men, babies and children. Too fat to run themselves, but living a dream through those racing by. Some of them wave flags: no favouritism, no patriotism – just admiration and wonder for the slender men rushing past. Some offer sweets and orange quarters, and are peeved when no one takes their gifts. Children try to touch an arm or vest of the fleet-footed heroes. A young boy half-heartedly holds out a piece of burger, smeared with relish. Relieved it is being ignored, he stuffs it into his mouth.

Many home fans, especially the blacks, support the new nation in southern Africa presided over by the legendary Nelson Mandela. And now it looks as if the three leading runners are from Mandela's rainbow nation.

CHAPTER EIGHTEEN

It is not to be. At the 17-mile marker, after leading for a couple of miles, two of the front runners pay the price for their boldness. They fall back and are swallowed up by the field, like seashells covered by the incoming tide.

But wait. To the surprise of many, it is the little black man who has stayed in front. Just! By no more than a second, the skin of his teeth. On his heels are no fewer than eighteen runners, waiting like cheetahs to spring on their tired quarry.

Sam has to do something. Victory is slipping away. He recalls chasing scavengers in the veld, running down jackals with his cunning. He'd slow down and then, when they thought they'd shaken him off, he'd suddenly make a burst: slow down, spurt; slow down, spurt. That often broke their spirit before he broke their necks.

He remembers Uncle Sabata's stories of Spiridon

Louis and Abebe Bikila, who never gave up. Slowly but surely, they wore down their opponents.

He may not win, but he'll do all he can to upset the rhythm of his rivals. It is now or never!

Calling on all his reserves and with a determined shake of his dreadlocks, he suddenly kicks hard and increases the pace. He covers the three miles between markers 18 and 21 in a punishing fifteen minutes. The effort is enough to shake off all but five of the chasing pack.

As he passes the 22-mile marker, he hears what he dreads most: footsteps behind him. A quick sideways glance tells him it is the Kenyan. The two Africans now run side-by-side, just ahead of a Korean runner. They open up a short gap ahead of three others.

All that now remains are the three miles of road leading to the Olympic Stadium. Three miles. Fifteen minutes.

The three front runners are locked together in a struggle for the lead. Only two seconds separate them as they approach the stadium. The South African is still in front, but no matter how much he varies the pace, kicks-and-slows, he cannot shake them off. If only he can hold on. . . Not far now. His lungs are bursting, his legs are as heavy as rocks, his breath rasps in his throat. Every ounce of his body screams *STOP!*

Yet his will is still strong. *He has to make it.* For his President. For the black people of South Africa. See, if *I* can do it, so can *you!*

To a great roar from the waiting crowd, the three runners enter the arena within touching distance. Two and a half times round the track. That's all that's left. Less than a thousand yards, a thousand strides.

Now the brave Korean puts in a burst. It takes him past the Kenyan and he is breathing down the leader's neck. Surely he has to reel him in. . . Yet each time he tries to pass him, the little South African grits his teeth, finds extra resources from somewhere and keeps ahead.

He breasts the tape a mere three seconds ahead of the Korean. It is the closest Olympic marathon finish of all time. He has beaten the best marathon runners in the world. His will to win has proved greater than theirs.

● ● ●

At the medal ceremony, in front of eighty-three thousand people in the arena, and billions more watching on television, his anthem, *Nkosi Sikelel'iAfrika* – 'God Bless Africa' – is played for the first time in athletic history. As he stands tall on the winner's rostrum, Samuel watches his country's new flag climb right to the top of the flagpole, and he sings out the words of the anthem. Loudly, proudly, triumphantly. His heart pounds even harder than it did during the race.

This moment is one of the most emotional ever, not only for South Africans. Round the world, millions of people cheer Sam's victory; thousands weep openly for the young son of Africa who has overcome the odds to be the best. His victory means far more than a gold medal. It is a symbol of justice for all, black as well as white.

Epilogue

Far away, in a little village in Bantustan, a party is taking place on the green. The Chief is in royal regalia. His dozen counsellors are wearing their faded pinstriped suits. Mother Priscilla and the other wives and children are singing and dancing in celebration. Their man has won.

Raising his pewter mug, the Chief says solemnly in a loud voice, 'I give you my son, the warrior.' Then he adds, half to himself, 'I knew he'd be champion one day.' Quickly, he raises the mug to his lips to hide the tears of pride rolling down his cheeks.

● ● ●

In a little round house outside the village, a young mother, her transistor radio playing full blast, is hugging her four daughters and smiling widely.

'That's your daddy,' she cries. 'He's champion of the world. He did it for you, for his brothers, Nicodemus and Looksmart, for all of us.'

● ● ●

In a neat bungalow not far from the township where he was born, a woman with straw-coloured hair, her cornflower-blue eyes shining brightly, turns to her two children. Pointing to the television, she says proudly, 'That's my friend. We won, comrade! We won!'

● ● ●

Many hundreds of miles away, on a hilltop overlooking Pretoria, a grizzled man in a jazzy gold shirt is dabbing his eyes with a white handkerchief as he paces up and down the presidential office. He never takes his eyes off the TV pictures of the black runner with the gold medal round his neck.

Turning to his wife, Nelson Mandela says in a hoarse voice, 'That, my dear, is the first black South African to win an Olympic gold medal. He is the first swallow of a glorious summer.'

● ● ●

Back in the Olympic stadium, grasping his gold medal, the champion's lips move silently, as if in prayer. He remembers what Nelson Mandela wrote in his book *The Long Walk to Freedom*.

He smiles guiltily.

Forgive me for changing your words, Madiba. I have *run* that long road to freedom. . .'

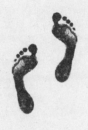

Note on Apartheid

In a scramble to divide up Southern Africa, the land was fought over by the British and the Dutch (also known as Afrikaners or Boers – the Dutch word for farmer). The Dutch had arrived in the seventeenth century. The discovery of gold in the 1880s attracted the British and, after two wars at the turn of the twentieth century, the British finally won. South Africa became part of the British Empire.

In 1910, the British and Afrikaners joined together in government and, by the Natives Land Act of 1913, took more than ninety per cent of the land for themselves. That left a mere seven point three per cent (later increased to thirteen per cent) for the native people. As a government minister put it at the time: 'The black man must be told that South Africa is a white man's country, that he is not going to be allowed to buy land there, and if he wants to be there he must be in service.'

Black protest had little impact against the might of white rule. But it did result in the setting up, in 1912, of the South African Native Congress, which became the African National Congress (ANC) in 1923.

If matters were not bad enough for non-white South Africans, they grew worse after 1 June 1948 when the Afrikaner Nationalist Party came to power. Right away it began to carry out a policy of Apartheid ('Apartness'), influenced by Hitler's 'Master Race' policies in Nazi Germany. As a result, every person was assigned to one of four categories:

> White (15 per cent of the population)
> Black (75 per cent)
> Coloured (mixed race – 7 per cent)
> Indian (3 per cent).

People were assigned to separate areas of the country, depending on their race. Most blacks were confined to the Bantu homelands. But to provide labour in the mines and factories (as well as cleaning and gardening), some blacks were permitted to live in what became known as 'townships' – slum shantytowns outside the white cities.

All non-whites had to carry a passbook which controlled where they could live and work. Most hotels, restaurants, libraries, colleges, buses – even park benches and beaches – were reserved for whites only. By this cruel, inhuman policy, even children's books with suspicious-sounding titles such as *Black Beauty* were banned.

Inspired by other African countries which achieved independence from their colonial masters, black South Africans, supported by some whites, began to fight back. The African National Congress drew up a Freedom Charter in 1955. It stated simply:

SOUTH AFRICA BELONGS TO ALL WHO LIVE IN IT, BLACK AND WHITE. . .

WE, THE PEOPLE OF SOUTH AFRICA, BLACK AND WHITE TOGETHER — EQUALS, COUNTRYMEN AND BROTHERS . . . PLEDGE OURSELVES TO STRIVE TOGETHER . . . UNTIL THE DEMOCRATIC CHANGES HERE SET OUT HAVE BEEN WON.

LET ALL PEOPLE WHO LOVE THEIR PEOPLE AND THEIR COUNTRY NOW SAY, AS WE SAY HERE: "THESE FREEDOMS WE WILL FIGHT FOR, SIDE BY SIDE, THROUGHOUT OUR LIVES, UNTIL WE HAVE WON OUR LIBERTY."

They won that freedom in 1994.

James Riordan is a children's writer and novelist, broadcaster, Russian scholar, retired association football player – and the first Briton to play football in the former USSR in 1963. He is also Visiting Professor at the University of Worcester, Emeritus Professor of Russian at the University of Surrey, and has been President of the European Sports History Association, as well as chronicling his time as a Communist footballer in *Comrade Jim: The Spy Who Played for Spartak*.

His first young adult novel, *Sweet Clarinet*, won the NASEN award and was nominated for the Whitbread Prize. *Match of Death* won the South Lanarkshire Book Award and *The Gift* was nominated for the NASEN award. His Frances Lincoln novels include *Rebel Cargo* and *The Sniper*, which was nominated for the Carnegie Medal.

He was Keynote Speaker at the 2002 South African Olympic Congress.

REBEL CARGO
James Riordan

Abena is an Ashanti girl sold into slavery
and transported on the notorious sea-route from
West Africa to Jamaica's sugar plantations. Mungo
is an English orphan who becomes a cabin boy,
only to be kidnapped and sold on as a white slave.
Mungo risks life and limb to save Abena from death,
and together they plan their escape to the
Blue Mountains, to a stronghold of runaways ruled
by the legendary leader Nanny. But can Mungo
and Abena get there before the Redcoats and their
baying bloodhounds drag them back. . . ?

Based on events and records of the time,
the novel unflinchingly describes conditions
of slavery in the early 18th century – a time when
profits took precedence over humanity –
and ends on a note of hope.

Chosen for the Boys Into Books must-read list –
"full of blood, guts and class heroes." *The Times*

"Fearlessly explores the cruelty and gruesome
reality of the slave trade while relating a truly
thrilling adventure story." *BookTrust*

"Riordan is a consummate teller of tales
for young people." *Amazon reviewer*

THE SNIPER

James Riordan

Stalingrad snipers were a legend in their time.
Their patience, keen eyes and ruthlessness helped
win the Battle of Stalingrad and turn the tide of
the Second World War. This is the true story of
a teenage sniper recruited in 1942 by Vasily Zaitsev
to seek out and shoot German officers. To begin
with, the youngster finds it almost impossible to kill,
but after a shocking discovery, goes on to 'snap as
many as 84 German sticks', and following capture
and a daredevil escape, leads a hand-picked unit on
a hazardous mission – to seize Field Marshall
Paulus, the Commander-in-Chief of
the invading army.

But this sniper is no ordinary marksman. . .

**"The lyrical opening must be one of the most
evocative in children's fiction. Riordan is a
consummate teller of tales for young people."**
Amazon reviewer

"Gripping." *Goodreads*

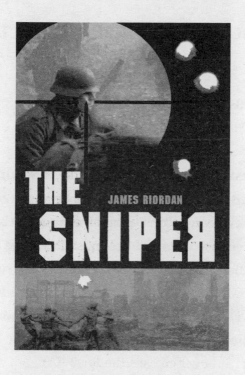

"A powerful and heart-rending story of
an ordinary girl in extraordinary circumstances."
School Librarian

"What makes this story compelling is that
the sniper, Tania Belova, is a girl." *Carousel*

"I for one could not put the book down. Riordan
does not shirk from presenting the cruelty and
hardship endured by the Russian people
and their enemies." *IBBY Link*

MORE BOOKS FROM FRANCES LINCOLN

BONE BY BONE BY BONE
Tony Johnston

The most important thing in David's life is his
friendship with Malcolm. In a secret ceremony in
a cave they even become blood brothers. But this
is 1940s Tennessee, and Malcolm is black. One day
David's fiercely racist father lays down a terrible
threat. If Malcolm ever enters their home, he will
kill him. David tries to change his daddy's mind,
but what will happen if Malcolm
ever crosses the line?

A powerful and haunting book, countering
the horror of racial hatred with a lyrical tribute
to childhood friendship.

**"A compelling, sometimes harrowing
coming-of-age story."**
Publishers' Weekly Starred Review

"A haunting future classic"
The Bookseller

THE BLUE-EYED ABORIGINE
Rosemary Hayes

It is 1629, and there is mutiny in the air aboard
the Dutch ship *Batavia* as she plies her way towards
Java with her precious cargo. Jan, a cabin boy, and
Wouter, a young soldier, find themselves caught up
in the tragic wrecking and bloody revolt that follow.
But worse is to come. . .

Based on real events, Rosemary Hayes's gripping
story recaptures some of sea history's most dramatic
moments, linking the fates of Jan and Wouter with
discoveries that intrigue Australians to this day.

"A definite must-read."
Young Writers

**"Gives an excellent account of the wrecking of the
Batavia whilst telling a captivating tale."**
ReadPlus

"Intriguing, hard-hitting story."
Reading Upside Down

WHEN I WAS JOE
Keren David

It's one thing watching someone get killed.
It's quite another talking about it. But Ty does
talk about it. He names some ruthless people
and a petrol-bomb attack forces him
and his mum into hiding under police protection.
Shy loser Ty gets a new name, a new look and
a cool new image. Life as Joe is good. But the
gangsters will stop at nothing to silence him.
And then he meets a girl with a dangerous
secret of her own.

A completely irresistible and award-winning thriller
by an exciting new writer.

**"David is a believable writer, so good that you
never actually notice just how good because you
are far too busy turning the pages."**
The Sunday Telegraph

"A gritty and compelling thriller."
Book Nook, *The Independent on Sunday*

ALMOST TRUE
Keren David

Ruthless killers are hunting Ty. The police move
him and his mum to a quiet seaside town.
But a horrific attack and a bullet meant for Ty
prove that he's not safe yet.

On the road again, Ty's in hiding with complete
strangers. . . who seem to know a lot about him.
Meanwhile he's desperate to see his girlfriend Claire,
and terrified that she may betray him. Ty can't trust
his own judgement and he's making dangerous
decisions that could deliver him straight to
the gangsters.

A thrilling sequel to *When I Was Joe*, shot through
with drama and suspense.

Praise for *When I Was Joe*:

**"I was so gripped that I couldn't put it down
even to brush my teeth or run my bath."
Caroline Lawrence, author of the
*Roman Mysteries series.***